The Big Diogenes

and Other Stories From the Anthropocene

By

Alan Webb

ISBN: 978-1-7778384-0-9

thebigdiogenes@gmail.com

ABOUT THE AUTHOR

Alan Webb is an ordained minister in the Church of the Latter Day Dude. But as a Dudeist Priest he is a bit of a maverick. He prefers red wine to White Russians; Tom Petty to Creedence; soccer to bowling; and perhaps the greatest sacrilege of all, he likes The Eagles. He lives near Vancouver.

ACKNOWLEDGEMENTS

This book would not have been possible without the generosity and forbearance of my brother Chris.

for posterity, hopefully

CONTENTS

THE BIG DIOGENES

The first time Alex saw him he was standing in the bushes bordering the car park in front of The Marketplace. His black track pants were lowered and a long grey woollen sweater was concealing his ass. It was a sunny mid-morning, a steady stream of traffic was passing by on the adjacent four lane road.

It struck Alex as he neared him that he couldn't possibly be pissing on the shrubberies right there in full view of society at large. Perhaps he was simply a wild-haired bird fancier peering in at a nest of Juncos, unaware that his ratty old pants were sagging to such an embarrassing extent.

But when he noticed pedestrians approaching the man on the sidewalk were cutting him a wide berth, and the smell of sour piss stung his nostrils, it became clear that this was not so. The man was indeed unashamedly urinating on an Euonymus. Voluminously so.

Aghast, Alex looked quickly away from the sight of the dripping, steaming bush, and the man's exposed junk, and veered almost into traffic in order to avoid him.

Bloody hell.

Having seen The Pisser once, in subsequent weeks Alex began to notice him often.

Driving in his car, Alex would catch sight of him shambling along the sidewalk with a little white dog trotting at the heels of his battered cross-trainers. Waiting at stoplights he would watch them flagrantly disobeying Do Not Walk signs. Parking his car at the market he'd see the man sunning himself on a bench next to the sidewalk, his face turned to the rays like a heliotrope, the dog by his side.

Often other men of apparently similar socio-economic status gathered around the man and his dog at this bench, always in lively debate.

1

Alex wondered what they talked about with such evident passion. QAnon conspiracies and anti-vaxxer nonsense seemed likely. But possibly, given the area's demographics, there were darker subjects under discussion.

For the municipality had always been a wealthy one, long home to so many well-heeled caucasians it seemed to virtually embody the white rock for which it was named. But the past decade or so had seen such an influx of ultra-rich residents it could've served as a suitable location for the filming of an episode of Succession.

Recent years had also seen a corresponding rise in the number of people spending days lolling about in any public place that hadn't yet shooed them away. Everywhere you looked it seemed, exhausted armies of Aqualungs were sprawled on park benches or on street corners spitting out pieces of their broken luck.

Nights were witness to blanketed lumps sleeping in storefront doorways and ATMs. Or shadowy figures cruising darkened neighbourhoods on bicycles with night vision head lamps affixed to their foreheads like nocturnal cyclops hunting for whatever wasn't locked up or tied down.

The sight of The Pisser and these men gathering in animated discussion, like in some sort of public debating forum, intrigued Alex. And unnerved him too. Were these the equivalent of Ted Talks for the indigent? Or something more sinister? A conspiratorial assembly of low level criminals meeting in order to divvy up neighbourhoods and parking lots amongst themselves like territories to be serviced by sales reps, or in this case looted? Like The Godfather's meeting of the five families brought to its most proletarian manifestation? Capitalism's bottom rung?

Alex was keen to satisfy his curiosity on these points, but not so keen as to venture too closely to the men's confabs. There was something vaguely intimidating, even overtly threatening, in a grouping of such men in an environment where their very presence seemed to be a subliminal challenge to the area's more natural, well-heeled natives. It didn't require too paranoid an imagination to intuit from these gatherings some sort of conspiratorial basis. Quite possibly deranged plotting sessions for a coming class war.

In any event, Alex found his inquisitiveness overpowered by fear and guilt. And by disgust too. For when his curiosity once drew him close enough to eavesdrop on The Pisser and his friends, the pong of the un-washed men quickly dissuaded him. He'd had to flee for the refuge of the Marketplace and bury his nose in a bouquet of the most fragrant roses he could find.

But one unseasonably hot early June day while Alex was parking his car at the market, he noticed The Pisser approaching a burly chap in a MAGA hat exiting a white Chevy van. The truck was older, grimy, had a ladder bungeed to its roof, and was riding on balding snow tires. On its right rear door it bore a large red decal.

The men conversed loudly enough that Alex could overhear them. The Pisser was saying: "I saw your bumpersticker."

The man regarded him warily. "Yeah? What about it?"

"'I always notice that those who support abortion have been born - Ronald Reagan.'"

"So?"

"I always notice that those who would deny a woman access to es-sential medical care rarely care about these women's lives or the lives of their children once they've been born."

The man pushed past him.

"Fuck off," he said.

"Well, if you care so much about children, do you support progres-sive social welfare policies like affordable housing, universal Pre-K and daycare, increased funding for health care and education, and the equi-table redistribution of wealth through progressive taxation?" he called after him. "HOW ABOUT BEQUEATHING KIDS A LIVABLE PLANET?"

As the man hurried for the liquor store The Pisser shrugged, said aloud to himself, "I guess that's a no," and sauntered off to his bench and sat down next to the dog and lifted his face to the sun and closed his eyes.

Alex found this exchange too intriguing to ignore. These were views he might have expressed himself if he'd shared The Pisser's impertinence. It appeared they might have something in common after all. So with an effort he mastered his inherent aversion to the lower classes and followed The Pisser to the bench by the road to speak to him.

"Hello," he said, looking down on him.

"Hello," The Pisser answered, not opening his eyes.

"My name's Alex."

"Hello Alex," he said, adding nothing further.

"I overheard your argument with that MAGA man. Good for you."

"I don't know that it was good or bad for me. And it wasn't any kind of argument. I just tried to engage the guy in debate and he wasn't interested."

"I don't think it was because he wasn't interested. I suspect the sum total of his argument was expressed in the bumper sticker and the 'fuck off.' So good for you for calling that man out as an imbecile. I always notice those who quote Ronald Reagan with approval are imbeciles."

"I don't know whether the man was an imbecile or not. His taciturnity prevents me from judging him one way or the other. It could be evidence of a kind of wisdom in itself I think."

"Well, I suppose that might be possible," Alex allowed, unconvinced. "But he looked a right berk to me."

The Pisser made no reply to this and simply sat with his eyes closed to the sun, seemingly not too fussed about engaging Alex further in conversation.

"What's your dog's name?" he asked finally after an uncomfortably long silence.

"Diogenes."

"Diogenes? Diogenes the Dog?"

This rang a bell with Alex, but one too faint for him to identify.

"That's a different sort of name for a dog."

"It's what he answers to."

"Hello Diogenes," Alex cooed at the dog. The dog ignored him.

"He doesn't seem to answer to it."

"How can you tell?"

"He didn't look at me when I used it."

"He didn't look because he's blind."

"Oh." Alex noticed now that the dog's eyes were indeed clouded. "Sorry."

"Don't be. He's not self-conscious."

Alex laughed. The Pisser didn't.

"What's your name anyway?"

"Apeman."

4

"No seriously."

"I am serious. It's what *I* answer to."

"But what's the name on your driver's license or on your ..." he was going to say pay cheque, then was about to substitute welfare cheque, but caught himself.

"What's your christian name?"

"I'm not a Christian."

"Okay, what were you called at birth?"

"Baby boy."

This was going nowhere. Alex wondered why the man was suddenly so reticent with him when he seemed only too eager to engage other much more humble characters in conversation. But strangely, The Pisser's demurrals only increased Alex's interest in talking to him.

"How long have you had him then? Diogenes?"

"He doesn't belong to me."

"Oh. I always see you together, so I just assumed. Who does he belong to?"

"Like all of us, he belongs to himself."

This seemed to Alex a dubious proposition, but he ignored it.

"Hi, Diogenes," he tried again. No response.

"He's not deaf too is he?"

"No."

"Only he didn't respond to that either."

"Maybe he doesn't think you're worth listening to."

"I see. Okay, if you're going to insult me ..."

"I didn't insult you. I was just positing a likely explanation for why he might not respond to your greeting. If anything it's him that's insulting you. Though I doubt that, he's a very amiable dog. It could be he's just hungry. Hunger can cause all sorts of anti-social behaviour."

"Oh I'm sorry. Is there anything I can do?"

The Pisser opened his eyes for the first time and in the shade cast by Alex's eclipse looked into his silhouette and suggested with the relish of a man who'd waited his entire life to do so, "You could get out of my sun."

"Oh, right. Terribly sorry."

Alex stepped a full stride to his left until The Pisser's face was lit.

5

"Hang on," he said.

Somewhere deep in his memory a tiny little steel ball of long unused education was circling a hole, about to drop into place. Plop. There.

"Diogenes the Dog? Apeman? Apemantus, you mean. That's Shakespeare. Timon of Athens. And Diogenes … he was that Greek philosopher who lived in a wine barrel and …" his voice trailed away as he decided suddenly it was probably better not to mention any of the other things Diogenes was famous for.

The Pisser opened his eyes and looked at him.

"And what?" he said.

"And uh, and lived an unconventional life," Alex stammered.

The Pisser smiled and once more turned his face to the sun and closed his eyes.

"So are you some sort of philosopher too?"

"Aren't we all?"

"Not even remotely. I don't know my Aristotle from my Zeno. And I was at Oxford."

"'To philosophize is to learn how to die,'" the Pisser quoted. "And we all learn how to die in the end. Nobody has ever got it wrong."

"That's very good. Who said that?"

The Pisser opened his eyes and looked round theatrically.

"I think I did, didn't I?"

"No, I mean originally. Because I think I've heard that before."

"The first bit was Montaigne, citing Cicero and Socrates. The last part was my own invention."

Alex grinned at him in astonishment.

"I'm astonished," he said. Told you. "What on earth are you doing here?"

"Well, as far as I know there are no other planets capable of sustaining life. And I have to be somewhere. So here I am. I can't think why that should seem astonishing."

"No, it's just that …"

A multitude of responses and possible questions arose for selection in Alex's mind like the show of hands of a highly engaged English boarding school classroom all waving for attention, ooh ooh, sir, sir. But before he could settle on what he wanted to say he was interrupted by the appearance of three of The Pisser's regular interlocutors.

"S'up Apeman?"

"Hello, Dude. Morning, Rog. John, how's it going?"

"Not too bad. Beautiful day, flush with money, perfect day to demonstrate the concept of free will," said John.

"John, don't fucking start that shit man. I will leave, I swear. I will fucking walk away right now," said Dude.

"I'm not starting anything. Just saying. I won a hundred and seventy bucks on Keno yesterday and nothing promotes free will like a wad of cash. Let's get some beers and head over to the park. We can talk about whatever you want Dude."

"Logical positivism?"

"No. Shut up, Rog."

"Take it easy John," said Dude. "Anyway, I gotta be at the Rec Centre in an hour for my second shot. But after that I'm free. No offence Apeman."

"None taken. You still misunderstand the concept."

"You're Pfizer aren't you Dude?" asked Rog.

He nodded while sparking up a joint.

"I was supposed to get the other one, but they gave me Moderna instead. Or maybe it was the other way around."

"Yeah, yeah, Rog, we heard this before," John said impatiently. "They gave you AstraZeneca the first time, and Moderna the second. I'm sure we'd all find it a fascinating anecdote if we didn't happen to speak English.

Christ, it's all anybody can talk about these days - the bloody vaccine. You're all a bunch lab rats for the benefit of Big Pharma and Bill Gates. You're specimens in a giant experiment. You know that, don't you?"

Dude and Rog stared at the sidewalk and said nothing. The Pisser frowned at the sun.

In the ensuing silence John noticed there was a tall sunburnt man with a long mane of white hair standing amongst them.

"Who are you stranger?"

"Me?"

The question caught Alex off guard. He was busy being horrified by the realization that he'd forgotten his mask in the car. He glanced around at them in mute alarm.

ALAN WEBB

John was a tall, corpulent fellow in his middle fifties or so, wearing
work boots, cargo shorts, a Hawaiian shirt, aviator sunglasses, and the
scowling expression of a man for whom the term bully was not a pejora-
tive. Rog was a small, reedy-looking chap with the timid look of a guy
forever on the lookout for a place to hide. And the geezer they called
Dude was a man clearly emulating Jeffrey Lebowski, sporting long hair,
shades, bushy Vandyke, Bermuda shorts, a tee shirt stretched over a middle aged paunch, and sandals.

None of them, including The Pisser, were wearing masks.

"My name is Alex."

"You from England?" asked Rog.

"Originally. I live here now. Have done for years."

"You look kinda familiar. Weren't you on TV? Didn't you used to
be on the news or something?"

"Well, I was on TV now and again I suppose. But not reporting the
news, no."

But he had been on TV! They all grinned at him, suddenly impressed and respectful. All but The Pisser, who remained, as before,
ignoring him, focused solely on basking in the sun.

"Oh, I know! You're that guy that makes nature shows aren't you?"

Alex smiled. "No, sorry to disappoint, but no."

"So what did you do? Were you a soccer player?"

"No Rog, for christ's sake. How would we recognize him if he was
a fucking soccer player?" said John. "You were an actor," he concluded,
sure of himself.

"I was a musician."

Dude lowered his glasses and scrutinized him with interest.

"What's yer name man?"

"Alex Watts. I was in a band called …"

"Wattage. Far out."

"Indeed. You've heard of us?"

"Sure, man. Of course."

"You're Alex Watts? From Wattage?" said John, amazed. "Holy shit.
Ho-lee shit. You are too! What are you doin' here?"

"Well, as your friend here said to me," he said, indicating The Pisser,
"I have to be somewhere, so here I am."

8

"We saw you at The Coliseum in '88," said John. "Remember Dude?"

Dude inhaled mightily and nodded and grunted happily in the affirmative.

"In '88? Yes, I think I remember that tour, sure. That would've been the Alimony Tour. Bit of a fog for me now I'm afraid. How were we?"

"It looked like you were having a good time."

"Yeah, you remembered most of the lyrics," said Rog.

"Did I? Jolly good."

"So you live here now?" said Rog. "I thought you lived in Spain or something. Or was that Alan Parsons?"

"No. Or rather yes, Alan does live in Spain. But I don't. Never have. I've lived here for years. Since the nineties."

"This is unreal," said John. "Dude, isn't this wild? Alex Fucking Watts. All this time we've been living *this* close to Alex Fucking Watts."

"Yeah. It's pretty cool, I have to say. I'm a fan, man. You had some great tunes."

"Thank you very much. One never tires of hearing that I assure you."

"We should do, like, one of those Reddit things. Ask me anything. You know? Can we do that?" said Rog. "Can we ask you some questions?"

"I'd be delighted. What would you care to know?"

The three looked at each other, stumped for an answer. Or for a question for that matter.

"True or false?" asked The Pisser. "'To show a rare and extraordinary excellence in frivolous pursuits is unworthy of a man of honour.'"

The three stooges looked abashed. John tried to shush him with a sotto voce "Ape!"

"False," volunteered Alex. "Decidedly false."

The Pisser opened his eyes and turned them toward Alex. "Go on ..."

"You're quoting Montaigne about Alexander the Great's love of chess aren't you? And I suppose insinuating that music is a frivolous pursuit? Well, I couldn't disagree more. What could be unworthy about making music? Music is simply an expression of joy, of harmony, of beauty. It's the wonder of existence made manifest. And it's a solace too for the times when life seems hardly bearable.

If Hamlet had ever heard Moonlight Sonata, or Fur Elise - or All You Need is Love, for that matter, he could never have conceived of the Earth as a sterile promontory, or the sky as a foul and pestilent congregation of vapours. Music is sublime. It makes life worth living. And what's more, it's simply a pleasure. And what could be dishonourable about such a simple innocent pleasure?"

The three nodded in agreement and turned to The Pisser for a reply. None was forthcoming. He merely offered what appeared a pitying smile, closed his eyes and turned them to the sun.

"Fuckin' A," said John, accepting the joint from Dude. "Here's to fuckin' pleasure."

"All You Need is Love?" said Rog, "Is that the greatest Beatles song, you think?"

"Off the top of my head. There were so many. But it does seem the quintessential 60's song doesn't it? The Side One, Track One, of any soundtrack of the age?"

"So you were a Beatles fan too? Just like us?"

"Yes of course. If you love music you have to be a Beatles fan. Just as you have to be a fan of Bach or Beethoven or Mozart."

"Did you know them?"

"I'm not quite old enough to have known Bach, Beethoven, or Mozart. But I did know the Beatles, yes."

"No kidding? And they knew you too? Like, to talk to?"

"Sure. We played the same tours and venues around England in the early days. We played Top of the Pops and Ready, Steady, Go!, with them a couple of times. And in London we all frequented the same clubs and bars. The Stones, the Hollies, the Animals, the Moody Blues, various actors, and artists, and assorted peerage progeny, we all hung out together. The Beatles too."

They gawped at him evincing the sort of reverential attitude the Fabs must've once shown awaiting the granting of a mantra by the Maharishi. Like he was a conduit for some otherworldly, mystical, higher truth. As though he'd been a witness at the Sermon of the Mount rather than merely chasing the same birds in various London clubs fifty-odd years before.

"There's no need for you to be too impressed," Alex said, amused by their beatific miens but wishing to tamp down their awe somewhat.

"They weren't born the Beatles you know. They weren't the issue of an immaculate conception, or of some other dubious mythic provenance. They were just supremely talented creative artists and insatiably curious human beings.

It was an enormously interesting and revolutionary period in history and they channelled the spirit of a wonderful golden age better than most. Them and Bob and Joni and a few others. It was a privilege to know them all as far as I did, but they were simply ordinary people touched by a very specific gift of genius."

"Romantic utopian bullshit," The Pisser scoffed from the bench, not bothering to turn his head Alex's way, nor even to open his eyes.

"What's so wrong about romantic utopianism? What's so wrong about imagining an ideal human society and trying to help make it come about? What could be more important than that?"

"Nothing at all. But you talk like the 60's were a glorious golden age of peace, love, and understanding when it was actually a dismal time of war, and assassinations, and CIA coups, and political repression. While you were wearing flowers in your hair and singing about love, most of the rest of the world spent the decade having a boot stamped on its face."

"I'm not saying the world wasn't an Orwellian nightmare in those days too. But we weren't just tripping and fucking. We protested. We tried to change the world. We tried to use our fame for the betterment of mankind.

John wrote Revolution. Joni wrote Woodstock. Stills wrote For What its Worth. Neil wrote Ohio. Bob wrote The Times They Are a-Changin,' and A Hard Rain's a' Gonna Fall, and Masters of War. Fogerty wrote Fortunate Son ..."

"Somebody wrote Hey, Hey, We're the Monkees ..."

"And somebody wrote Yummy Yummy Yummy and Sugar Sugar too. So what? We used our talents and what influence we had for good. We did what we could. And no one can say we didn't make a difference."

"Your defensiveness argues otherwise."

"I have nothing to be defensive about."

"No? Tell me, I forget now, what was your contribution to the great soundtrack of the revolution?"

"I wasn't really a political artist in that sense. Some wrote from a more didactic, socio-political standpoint. And some tried to transform

11

society by inspiring personal change, a transformation of individual consciousness. That was my way. I wrote about life and love, and my perceptions of my own reality."

"From what I can remember that seems a generous way of describing your music. Self-indulgent caterwauling is what I recall."

"Well, perhaps. But self-indulgent caterwauling in pursuit of a higher purpose, thank you very much."

"You were filler between radio ads. You were the products of corporate marketing campaigns and dimwitted consumer culture. Nothing personal. I'm not just talking about you, but of all your fellow 'legends' too. You were just the crap peddled to young people to indoctrinate them into consumerism. You were Neo-liberalism's dupes. Capitalism's cuddly shock troops. You were cooler than mom's soap powder or dad's deodorant or Tang drink crystals. You sold blue jeans and Coke and endless wars of white western colonialism. All sound and protest, signifying nothing but profits and increased market share."

"Ape, c'mon man," said Dude. "Take it easy."

The Pisser shrugged nonchalantly, as if to say, I'm just being honest, man.

"No, it's alright," Alex insisted. "You had to be there, that's all. Something was happening and you just didn't know what it was Mr. Jones.

We saw a world that cried out for changing, and set out to try. We felt all of history had been leading up to that moment in time and that all of our passion and idealism was making possible a new age for mankind and that we could somehow achieve a kind of heaven on earth for everyone. No more wars and violence and conflict. No more greed and poverty and discrimination."

The Pisser smiled sardonically. "How did that work out then?"

"That may all seem hopelessly naive now, I'll grant you. But at the time we thought we were on to something righteous. And we did change the world, I'm convinced of it, if only a little."

"Blue jeans and Coke," replied The Pisser simply. "Chevrolet and MasterCard and McDonnell Douglas."

"No. I don't agree. It wasn't a mirage. It wasn't all for nought. We saw a world mired in a dismal, stultifying, self-denying ethos that seemed to reject the idea that life should be a joy and a pleasure. A society that chose instead, out of guilt or misperceived duty or obligation, to live life like it was a sentence to be served for the sin of being born. And we said, no. Life should be a dance, not drudgery.

And I think that spirit, some of that idealism, survived us. Our kids and grandkids are busy today taking up the fight. I like to think we Boomers inspired that much, if nothing else."

"Oh please. You Boomers were a bunch of rich white kids living in your rarefied paradises playing silly buggers for filthy lucre."

"'You Boomers?' How old are you? Don't point the finger at me or some compromised, rapacious 'us.' We didn't make our money peddling fossil fuels like drug lords to a world full of desperate oil-craving junkies, and then systematically lie about the health and environmental effects of that addiction for decades. We simply made music and films and art about peace and love and the meaning of life and the human condition."

"Empty words," said The Pisser. "You absorbed the mass's genuine desire for protest and change and echoed back at them superficial phrases of dissent and a kind of Potemkin protest movement. And just as progress beckoned you retreated to your mansions and counted your loot.

You didn't end war and violence, you watched as it became ubiquitous, an entertainment business in itself. You didn't raise the collective consciousness, you raised profits and share prices. You didn't bring power to the people, you ennobled capitalism."

"Just out of curiosity, what should we have done? Taken up guns rather than guitars? Made more corpses instead of music? I studied Oscar Peterson at school, not Karl Marx. My music may have bored you to death, but apart from killing somebody softly with my song, that was the only way I was going to purposely end someone's life."

"You were the first so-called 'influencers.' You had enormous power over the popular imagination. If any sort of egalitarian utopia was possible for humanity you may very well have brought it about. But you sold it, and us, out instead."

"That is absolute bollocks. You just painted us all as mercenary charlatans and ludicrous egotists playing pantomime revolutionaries. And now you're arguing that our sin wasn't that we were playing at being revolutionaries, it was that we were bad at it? Have I got that just about right? And who said anything about egalitarian utopias anyway?"

"I believe you did, in so many words. And blame is going to be cast, you wait. You rich Boomers are going to have to wear it. Your heaven on earth has descended into a spiralling, waking nightmare and the ones whose future you sold out for your posh lifestyles and investment port-folios are going to come back at you seeking their full share of vengeance. Be warned."

Alex took a step back on his heels and shook his head as if he'd taken an Ali jab to the temple.

"Bloody hell. I didn't expect a kind of Spanish Inquisition. I was just on my way to the store. We were out of yogurt. Give me a hit on that thing will you," he said, reaching for the joint.

Dude obliged.

"Are you guys just going to stand there? I thought you were going to be the comedy relief."

All at once, as if on cue, Diogenes sprung to life, jumped to the ground and trotted into the shrubberies to lift his leg. All but Apeman watched with apparent interest. When he was finished he hopped back up on the bench and put his head down on his front paws, Sphinx-like.

"Ladies and gentlemen, the comedy stylings of Diogenes," said Dude. "For a dog you can't beat him for pithy commentary."

"More like pissy commentary I'd say," said John.

They shared the joint around in silence for a time while Alex con-templated a way to make a face-saving retreat. At length Dude popped the last remnants of the roach into his mouth and swallowed it.

"What time is it getting to be John?" he asked.

John consulted his phone. "It is … nine-forty-seven and thirty-eight seconds. Thirty-nine seconds. Forty …"

"Okay, got it. I gotta go now or I'll miss my shot."

"What time's your appointment Dude?" asked Rog.

"Ten."

"You'll never make it in … however many minutes that is."

"I've got a car. I can give you a ride," Alex volunteered, seeing a ready exit.

"Fuckin' A man. The Dude abides. Where ya parked?"

Alex and Dude headed for the car and the others trailed after them, including Apeman and Little Diogenes. Alex had no problem sharing his car with Dude, or with Walter and Donny - sorry, John and Rog, for that matter. But the debate still rankled. And there were other reasons too why riding with The Pisser and Diogenes was not an appealing proposition.

Alex's car was a BMW i3, a vehicle so small it might've been designed to disgorge a multitude of clowns at a circus. When they reached it he thought perhaps its size would convince at least The Pisser and Diogenes into a change of plans. But no.

John took the front passenger seat, and Dude, Rog, and Apeman squeezed into the backseat, with Little Diogenes assuming the Sphinx pose on Ape's lap.

A foul stench immediately enveloped the car. Alex lowered all the windows and opened the sunroof and put on the mask that had been hanging on the rearview mirror.

Carefully he backed out of the stall and joined a slow stream of cars circling the lot in search of the ever elusive parking spot closest to the entrance. Their progress was almost instantly halted as two drivers attempting to nose into one space conducted a profane argument in vigorous semaphore. After waiting for tens of seconds, John suggested forcefully that Alex drive up on the sidewalk to get around them.

"I can't do that," Alex insisted.

"Sure you can. There's no one coming. Drive up on the curb."

"No. It's not done. There are rules."

"What? Principles of parking lot etiquette? It's not fucking anarchy. Just go man. Drive up on the curb! Dude'll be late!"

John grabbed for the wheel and wrenched it sharply to the right. With his left foot he stamped on Alex's right pedal foot. The car lurched forward and the passenger's side wheels jumped up on the sidewalk while Alex frantically tried to steer in a more or less safe, straight ahead fashion. Horns sounded. Voices shouted. The little clown car raced along the sidewalk, descended a wheelchair ramp to the blacktop, scooted smoothly across the pavement, and then ascended the ramp to the walkway on the opposite side of the lane, careening madly past stationary cars on their left, patiently lined up, abiding by the unwritten laws of parking lot ethics.

"Sorry!" Dude placatingly called out the window.

Suddenly there were pedestrians standing directly in their path. Only, no, they weren't pedestrians, they were a group of protestors brandishing signs and chanting outside the liquor store's entrance.

'Baby Killers' read one sign. 'Masks Kill' read another. Faces immediately turned on them, mouths shaped in terrified "O" configurations. One of them was the MAGA man from The Pisser's earlier verbal contretemps, holding a placard depicting a large syringe jabbing a crudely drawn sheep.

"Shit!" yelled Alex.

"What the fuck!" bellowed MAGA man as he and his half dozen fellow Covidiots scattered madly off in all directions.

"Sorry!" shouted Alex as they passed.

Finally free of the logjam Alex regained control of the car and his self-possession and they managed to exit the parking lot onto the street in a more or less sedate fashion. The two blocks between the mall and the Rec centre passed mercifully by without incident and they rolled to a stop outside the entrance just in time for Dude to sprint inside to make his appointment.

While Dude was getting jabbed, Alex parked the car next to a soccer field and suggested they get out and sit on the grass in the blessedly fresh air while they waited.

John requested some music other than the Leonard Cohen Alex had been listening to, and it was agreed amongst them, with The Pisser's abstention, that it was So Long Marianne. Harmony was achieved when they collectively determined to get High in the Morning with Tom Petty's satellite channel instead.

As Alex, John, Rog, and The Pisser laboriously lowered themselves to the ground, Little Diogenes sauntered over to the centre circle and crapped at almost the precise spot on the halfway line where play would kick off when organized team sports were allowed again.

"That is a remarkable coincidence," said Alex, watching him.

"What's that?" said Rog, sparking up another doobie.

"He defecated right on the centre spot! Of all the acres of empty grass to squat, he chose that one. That's amazing."

"Why is it so remarkable or amazing that any ordinary bodily function be carried out at any particular place?" enquired The Pisser.

"You would say that, wouldn't you?" Alex replied, wrinkling his nose in half-anticipation of being struck by an olfactory memory of his first sight of him. "But you know what I mean, surely. Firstly, he's called

Diogenes, a dog named for an historical figure who was infamous for doing the full range of his bodily functions wherever he pleased, in public. That is something of a coincidence at the very least.

And secondly, it's like he walked into a bar, picked up a dart, threw it blindly at a wall and not only hit a dart board, but nailed a bullseye! And, to reiterate, he's bloody blind! And he's a dog! Even if he were neither of those things that must surely count as an amazing coincidence!"

"It can't be a coincidence that a dog should defecate in a public place. Where else would you expect him to go?" reasoned The Pisser reasonably. "And secondly, if you have an infinite number of dogs who shit at random in an infinite number of public places, one of them is bound to crap on a soccer field's centre spot eventually."

"He's only one dog."

"Yes, but he does shit an awful lot."

"Well I still say there are stranger things in heaven and Earth than are dreamt of in your infinite dog-shitting theorems."

"What in god's holy name are you blathering about?" said John, accepting the joint, inhaling prodigiously, and passing it on to Alex. He then laughed, snorted, and farted simultaneously, before stretching out on his back on the grass.

"To see him high in the morning and by evenin' see him gone …" sang Tom.

"What do you get when an infinite number of assholes cut an infinite number of farts?" John straight-manned.

"FOX News?" answered Rog. "The Republican Party?"

"I don't know," answered John. "I was asking you."

"Oh. I thought you were making a joke."

"I was. I couldn't think of a punchline. I thought one would come to me organically once I was in pressing need of one."

"How about global warming?" Rog suggested.

"Global warming? That's your idea of a punchline?"

"No, that wasn't a punchline. I thought maybe you were being … I'm confused. Methane gas and global warming. That's what you get with infinite farts. Like with cows."

"Okay, you've lost me now. Anyway, it's a hoax!"

"What? Cows, or methane gas?"

"No. How could cows be a hoax? Global warming."

"Oh no," Alex groaned, offering the reefer to The Pisser. "You're not one of those too are you?"

"One of what?"

The Pisser declined. He passed it to Rog.

"A climate change denier and an anti-vaxxer."

"I am not a climate change denier." John said. "I'm not an idiot. I was being facetious."

"Oh good, I'm very relieved to hear it."

"But those vaccines are evil man. The pandemic is nothing but a secret plot to stop population growth."

Alex laughed.

"You think I'm joking?"

"You mean you're not?"

"No."

"Oh god, let there be a change in topic."

"It's true, I'm not kidding. I saw this documentary on YouTube that proved that there's a cabal of Democrats, and Big Pharma, and left wing global elites like Bill Gates, and Barack Obama, and George Soros, and George Clooney and his Arab wife, who're all trying to stop global warming by population control. It's all based on this Malthus guy who predicted in the 1800's or something, that out of control population growth would lead to global famine and nuclear wars and a bunch of other bad shit."

"You've just heard yourself say that out loud. Does any of that sound even remotely true to you? I mean seriously, Malthus warned of nuclear war in the 1800's? That would be truly extraordinary. Like Trump lauding the Revolutionary Army for securing the airfields in 1776."

"It's true. Google it. Do your own research, man. They cooked up the virus with the help of their Commie buddies in that Chinese lab and let it loose so they'd have the excuse to inject us all with some kind of sterilizing agent."

"Uh huh. Just out of curiosity, were you planning to have kids at your age?"

"You never know. Probably not I guess."

"So what's your problem with the vaccine then?"

"That's not the point. It's fucking wrong. It's an outrage. They're trying to take away our freedom to procreate. You should be angry too. This is the most heinous medical thing since Nazi doctors, and all you sheeple are just going along with it, lining up to get your shots like good little … I don't know whats. Here, I'll show you."

John took out his phone, tapped at it madly, and held it out to Alex. He waved it away.

"I'm surprised you use those things John. What with the 5G and all, and you keeping it stashed so close to your gonads. Doesn't that phone threaten some sterilizing effects?"

John looked at the phone in his hand and then at Alex, but couldn't seem to form a reply.

"Look, I'll tell you what," Alex said, "if I promise to Google it later when I get home can we agree to change the subject to something a little more … sane. Sorry, no offence, but I couldn't think of a more appropriate word."

John turned on Rog, and growled, "Don't Bogart that thing Peter Lorre."

Rog handed the joint over and John took several long hits and passed it to Alex.

"Like I said Alex, do your research man. Don't take my word for it. Check out Facebook and YouTube. There's tons of good information there. Real doctors and professors and such. Top top nerds and geeks."

"From Trump University no doubt. Now, a change of topic, I beg of you. And nothing referencing the letter Q, Hilary Clinton, or Democratic Party pedophilia rings if you please."

Alex's provisos seemed to have the immediate effect of casting them into thoughtful silence. What was there to talk about if the batshit mental was excluded?

The sound of simple piano chords, played slowly, almost hesitantly, emanated from the car. In response, in unison, they all stretched out on their backs on the grass to listen and ruminate and stare up at the vast cloudless blue sky as Tom Petty began to sing:

> 'It's good to be king, if just for a while/ To be there in velvet, yeah, to give 'em a smile/ It's good to get high and never come down/ It's good to be king of your own little town …'

"You know what this reminds me of?" said John, finally. "Linus and Charlie Brown lying on the grass staring up at the sky, and Linus sees some fancy smart-ass shape like Rodin's The Thinker or something in the clouds, and asks Charlie Brown what he sees. 'I see a horsey and a ducky' he says."

Rog and Alex laughed.

"Actually, I don't see any clouds at all," said Alex.

"There are always clouds, whether you can see them or not," said The Pisser. "More and more every day as increasing heat evaporates ever more water and creates ever more heat-trapping water vapour, which in turn evaporates ever more water, etcetera, etcetera, in a vicious negative feedback loop of global heating ending in our extinction."

"Thud," said Alex. "That just brought us back down to Earth."

"It's just reality."

"Yes, well, reality is a nightmare from which I am trying to awake."

"Ah, Stephen Dedalus. Very appropriate," said The Pisser. "A reference to a fictional character named for the father of Icarus, a boy who ignored wise counsel and the clear evidence of his own senses and native intelligence and flew too close to the sun. We're all going to get our metaphorical wings melted soon with runaway climate change. So I guess you could say the history of your failed 60's utopianism is another nightmare we're all trying to awake from too."

"Can we have another change of subject?" asked John. "Reality sucks. I'd rather argue about Q or Hilary Clinton than hear any more about fucking climate change. We all get it. We're fucked. *I'd* like to talk about something else. Anything else."

"My 60's utopianism?" Alex continued, propping himself up on one elbow and regarding The Pisser. "Judging by appearances I'd say you were there too. What did you do during the proverbial war, Apeman?"

"I dodged the draft of a very non-proverbial war."

"Seriously? said John.

"You're American?" asked Rog.

"Yes and yes. And my government tried to sacrifice me for a monstrous lie. To provide profits for arms manufacturers, and jobs and investment in swing states and corrupt politicians' congressional districts. They tried to kill me while you got high and sang love songs. So I burned my draft card and fled to Canada. That's what I did in the war."

"Oh, well, I see. I didn't know. I'm sorry."

"No need to apologize. I prefer it here. It's a much more civilized place. At least it was until we sold our souls for Tar Sands loot. Now we're as morally compromised as the worst of them. Co-conspirators in the ultimate crime against humanity."

"Ah, now I begin to understand. What's that old saw? A cynic is but a disappointed romantic? You've been in search of a utopian paradise all your life and they keep yanking it out from under your feet just when you think you've found it. Is that it?"

"First of all, I am not in any sense a romantic. And I'd classify myself as more of a Stoic than a Cynic. I've never believed a utopia was possible on Earth. We may be born innocent, but society is inherently corrupting. The best we can do is to try to live enlightened, rational lives. And there is nothing enlightened or rational in destroying the environment we depend upon to live."

"You are a Romantic! Born innocent? What's that but a reference to the Fall? And everything else you've said echoes the same theme too. Every word, in effect, doth almost speak your name. But that name isn't Shakespeare, to mix my bardic metaphors. It's Wordsworth. You may as well be reciting The World is Too Much With Us."

"I seldom wander lonely as a cloud. I just don't think it's a romantic notion that we shouldn't shit where we sleep and eat."

How about pissing where we shop? was the obvious retort here, but Alex controlled himself.

"So you would prefer a society that rewards good, selfless behaviour?" he said instead. "One that leads us ineluctably to choose to lead the kind of ethical, moral lives that will save us from climate change? A sort of rational, idealistic revolution of the individual to achieve a kind of reintegration of man and nature? A new heavenly existence in this world?"

"I wouldn't phrase it that way exactly. But yes, the alternative, it seems to me, is collective suicide."

"Indeed."

"Not that I would ever deny a person's inalienable right to personally off themselves. No one should have to suffer unendurable anguish. But I draw the line at mass self-slaughter. I have no idea where Wordsworth stood on that. Next to a lake gawping at daffodils probably."

"So people should be free to choose to kill themselves then?"

"I don't see why not. No one should have to suffer needlessly."

"Aha! Checkmate! That sounds like free will to me. A Romantic and a free willer! You stand revealed in all your naked innocence."

"No one freely chooses an existence so bereft of hope the only solution they can think of is to kill themselves. A million external factors and inherited genes and god knows what else go into those kinds of decisions. In fact, I'd say most decisions we make are pretty much preordained by nature or nurture. You, of all people, should be comforted by the absence of free will."

"Why is that exactly?"

"It gives you a ready excuse to duck responsibility for the profound mediocrity of your music. Though clearly, profound isn't the right word."

"Oh come on," insisted John. "'Catatonic Teatime'? 'Flexy Phoebe'? Fucking genius."

"Oh yeah," agreed Rog. "What about 'Head Cleaner'? That whole album was killer. Top Fifty all time, easy."

"How about 'What Was I Saying'? Fucking classic, man."

"You're too kind."

"Hey Alex, was 'Psychedelic Mind Wank' really about 'Their Satanic Majesties Request'?"

Alex laughed.

"I've heard that rumour, but no. It was said about a Floyd show back in Syd's day. And not by me unfortunately. It was a line I pinched from Keith. I liked it so much I stole it. That's just between us though. No doubt he has no recollection of ever saying it, but any lawyer worth his retainer would see a case for suing me for back royalties."

"Ah, there we are," said The Pisser, "any discussion of music inevitably segues into the topic of money. That is the essence of your musical career. A portrait of the artist as a greedy young man. You may as well have sold real estate or investment funds. You and all your mythologized peers. Nothing but a bunch of capitalist fifth columnists, the lot of you."

"Look Apeman," replied Alex wearily, "everyone has to survive somehow. Music was the only thing I could do, the only thing I had to offer the world. I was lucky. Most musicians, the vast majority of all artists in fact, do not make enough to survive on. So I don't know why I should feel any need to apologize to you for creating something that a lot of people were willing to pay for to enjoy. It seems a fair bargain."

"To you maybe."

"Sure, to me. But the odds were just as good, rather better in fact, that I would fail to find an audience at all and end up playing jazz standards in pretentious steak restaurants. Would you still be haranguing me then, in my failure? Or is it just success you have a problem with?"

"What I have a problem with is a decades long capitalist orgy raging while the world burns. Intentionally or not, you wallowed in that orgy."

"I was invited."

"Bully for you. I was a conscientious objector. When the doomed come searching for those to blame for a terminal world they won't be looking for me. They'll come for their revenge to the likes of you."

"Well, I won't be here."

"Aye, there's the nub. None of you cunts will be there when the bill comes in for the consequences of your sociopathic self-indulgence and pathological indifference to human life. You'll all have fled the scene."

"That's not what I meant."

"Maybe not. But I mean what I say."

"I still don't understand the point you're trying to make. What you're so disdainful of is simply human nature. It's only natural to seek comfort and pleasure, to pursue happiness. I don't know what you'd find acceptable. Would it be better if we hadn't developed the intellectual capacity and self-awareness to want to climb down from the trees in the first place?"

"Maybe."

"Well then we may as well go extinct. What good is a verdant planet free of beings without a consciousness capable of enjoying it?"

"There are different levels of consciousness. You don't think simians in trees enjoy their environment and their lives? Or beasts in the field, or birds in the trees?"

"Higher consciousness then. What good is a planet where a tree can fall in a forest and there's no one there to hear it?"

"They are there to hear it."

"Yes, they can experience it, but they can't express their understanding of it, the wonder of it, beyond beating their chests, or flinging their faeces, or flying off in alarm. What good is a heaven bereft of souls?"

"Oh god. Souls? You talk of souls? What century are we in?"

"A soul is the capacity for self-awareness, the capacity to express wonder through self-expression, art or language."

"Well Rock Star, because of the likes of you we're about to find out what good a heaven bereft of souls is really like."

"You know, Ape?" said John. "Sometimes you can be a real human paraquat."

"Because of the likes of …" began Alex angrily, before looking abruptly at John still lying stretched out on the grass.

"Wait a tick. Did you say human paraquat?"

"Yeah. It means …"

"I know what it means. The only other time I heard the term I looked it up. That was in The Big Lebowski. I knew it. What are you guys, a Big Lebowski tribute act?"

"The Big Lebowski? No, what's that?"

Alex looked at John's apparently face-less recumbent bulk.

"Are you quite serious?" he asked the hillock of torso.

"Totally. Why? What is it? Or who is it?"

"It's a film. And a character in that film. Played by Jeff Bridges. You've never seen The Big Lebowski?"

"No."

"I don't believe you."

"Suit yourself."

"The Dude? You've never heard of The Dude?"

"Dude's inside getting vaxxed," said Rog.

"You astound me," said Alex, and he laid back down on the grass.

There followed a long silence before, at last, Rog finally lost the struggle and emitted a barely perceptible titter.

"'COURSE WE'VE FUCKIN' SEEN IT!" John shouted. "Like a thousand times," and he and Rog exploded in long-suppressed laughter.

"You bastards. I thought you were having me on. I was beginning to think I was mad."

"We saw it in the theatre when it first came out," remembered Rog.

"By accident," said John. "We were stoned and got in the wrong line. Can't remember what we were wanting to see."

"Half-Baked," said Rog.

"What?"

"It was Half-Baked. That was the movie we wanted to see."

"Never heard of it. Anyway, I almost walked out in the first thirty seconds. When The Stranger is drawling the voice-over and the music is all weird and the tumbleweeds are blowing and all that? I thought, what the fuck is this? Dude convinced me to give it a chance, and the rest is history."

"Was he 'Dude' before that?"

"Oh no. From that moment on he was," said Rog. "But before that he was just Ray."

"Ray Darwin. Or Ray-J. 'You can call me Ray, and you call me Jay' …"

"Now it's just Dude. He had it legally changed when he was ordained."

"Ordained?"

"Uh huh. He's an ordained minister."

"Good lord. Of what church?"

"The Church of the Latter Day Dude."

"Are you quite serious? There's a church?"

"Yep. You send them twenty-five bucks and they send you back a certificate of ordination, a bumper sticker, and some Dudeism decals for your car window."

"And they worship Jeff Lebowski? A fictional character?"

"Worship is not the correct nomenclature," corrected John. "We follow the tenets of Dudeism. We don't worship. We take guidance from his example. The Tao of The Dude."

"But he's fiction. He never existed. The Coen Brothers invented him."

"No one really knows whether Jesus existed or not. He may have. But it's just as possible that it's all a myth invented by guys with their own agendas hundreds of years after he died. Or didn't die, depending on whether he ever really lived or not. We think he existed because they say he did. Well, where's the evidence?"

"The son of god, the virgin birth, the resurrection, water into wine, all that shit?" added Rog. "Come on."

"And what's Christianity got to do with what he's supposed to have preached anyway? All that meek inheriting the earth, and camel through a needle stuff? It's just the world's oldest and richest multi-national corporation now."

"Yeah. I think in a couple hundred years we're gonna be following the teachings of the Dude instead of Jesus or Mohammed or whoever. We'll probably go extinct if we don't."

"So are you two ministers as well? Or should I say disciples?"

"No. We're just Dude's parishioners."

"There's a parish?"

"Of course."

"Is there a church?"

"The world is our church."

"Quite right. And how many members are there in Dude's parish?"

John considered this for a moment, stroking his chin. Rog pursed his lips in concentration.

"About … five."

"If you include Dude."

"Yeah, including Dude. And Diogenes."

"And Diogenes. Oh, and Apeman."

"I belong to no church," said The Pisser, unequivocally.

"So, four. Or wait a moment. Is that three? Wanna join?" asked John.

"Would I have to tithe?"

"You can if you want to."

"I'll consider it. Would I have to bowl and drink Caucasians and listen to Creedence?"

"Good luck finding a bowling alley these days. We get together and play Keno in the mall," said Rog.

"And drink beer mostly. Vodka and Kahlua and milk? That's expensive."

"And we smoke weed."

"Well, weed, that goes without saying. Weed is the Word and the Way."

"Amen. Weed is the word, and the word is the way, we follow Dude's example, though we used to call him Ray," sang Rog.

"Jesus. We do need some custom-built hymns, but that's pretty bad."

"You try, John."

"Shut up Rog. We do listen to Creedence, though. They're cool. But we're mostly into Tom Petty."

"And The Eagles. I like The Eagles."

"Yeah, me too. I never got that part. Hating the fucking Eagles. I mean, 'Take it Easy'? Right? One of the central tenets of the faith. It doesn't make narrative sense."

"I always wondered at that myself," said Alex. "One of the eternal mysteries one presumes."

"Alex, maybe you could write us some hymns," suggested Rog.

"There's an idea!" agreed John. "How'd you like to write the score for the next great world religion?"

"That's an intriguing idea. But I don't, as a point of principle, have anything to do with religion. No offence, but my view of a belief in a supreme supernatural being is that it's absolute bosh. The most dangerous, destructive bosh there has ever been to be honest."

"But you'd just be writing the theme music, not endorsing the entire belief system. Was what's his name advocating for Jesus Christ when he wrote Superstar?"

"I've no idea. It wouldn't surprise me, actually."

"Okay, but how about when he wrote Cats? Was he endorsing some pro-feline religious doctrine when he wrote that crap? No. He was just putting his god … his talent to work in a totally undogmatic way so he could make great wads of cash."

"You're proposing to pay me then?"

"Well, not up front. But just think of the royalties you'll get for writing the theme track for the creed that finally replaces the supernatural superstitious doctrines with a species-saving faith devoted to the harmonious co-existence of nature and humankind."

"I'm nearly seventy-five. Is this going to happen any time soon?"

"Your wife and kids and their descendants will get the residuals. Until the end of time," said Dude.

Alex, startled, shaded his eyes and looked up to see Dude, en-haloed by the sun, standing suddenly above John and Rog. He hadn't noticed he was there. It was almost like he'd just materialized out of thin air. John and Rog and The Pisser seemed not in the least surprised.

"Well, when you put it that way …"

"You'll do it?" asked John.

"Sure. Why not. I haven't written anything in ages. It might be fun. Do you have any writings I can set to music? Or should I just watch the film again?"

"Rog had that thing earlier," said John doubtfully.

Alex laughed. "Okay. That's a place to start. Come on. I've got a home studio. Let's see what we can come up with."

**

Squeezing into the little car again, they set off, very, very cautiously for Alex's place, all but The Pisser loudly singing along with Tom Petty's 'Stayin' Alive (It's the Running Man's Bible'):

'It was not in my vision/ It was not in my mind/ To return from a mission/ A man left behind …'

After a couple of minutes journey, four lanes narrowed to two and cheek-by-jowl houses on small lots were replaced by briefly glimpsed mansions, security gates and long expanses of wall. As though not wanting to disturb the comfortable residents of these exclusive manors, the travellers fell into an apparent respectful silence not unlike peasants deferentially doffing their caps in passing to the landed gentry of Alex's native England.

The reverential hush went unbroken until Rog uttered an involuntary "whoa," as they passed through the parting gates leading to Alex's abode. At the foot of a long paving-stone drive past gardens as elaborate and colourful as an Impressionist show, lay a relatively modest-sized Tuscan-style villa. Alex brought the little BMW to a stop under the porte cochere.

"Nice shack," said Dude.

"Ta very much. Come on in."

Huge, arched, medieval-style, solid wooden double doors opened at their approach to present to their view a bronzed, statuesque blond of indeterminate age dressed in white shorts and matching blouse. She was just the sort of ageless goddess you'd expect a retired rock star to be married to. Beyond her and the cool airy great-room was a vision of nothing but sparkling azure sea.

"Holy," said Rog.

John immediately ran his hands over his head in a futile effort at neatening his dishevelled hair.

"There you are," she said kissing Alex, "I wondered where you'd got to. Who're your friends?"

"This is Rog."

"Hi."

"This is John."

"Ma'am."

"This is Dude."

"Hello."

"This is …oops," Little Diogenes sprinted through the door past them, "that was Diogenes. And last but not least, this is Apeman."

She reacted with the barest flicker of surprise at this, but quickly recovered and said with genuine warmth, "Well, it's a pleasure to meet you all. Come in, come in," she said.

"Everyone, this is my wife Cass."

They all repeated their greetings. Hello. Hello. Hello. Apeman nodded solemnly at her.

Meanwhile, Little Diogenes was tearing about the house in a frenzy, jumping on and off the furniture, circling the kitchen island like a dervish, galloping up and down the hall. As they moved thru the living room toward the patio the little dog attempted an emergency stop procedure on the ceramic tile floor and executed a four-paw slide directly into Cass's legs. She laughed and reached down and rubbed his exposed belly until she noticed. She shot a horrified glance at Alex. He guessed what was the matter and nodded discreetly toward The Pisser.

"Mister Apeman? We have a doggy shower downstairs that we haven't used for a while. Would you mind if I gave little Diogenes a bath?"

"Diogenes belongs to no man," said Alex, "he may choose to act from his own free will. Isn't that right?" he asked The Pisser.

"As far as it goes," Ape said. "That'd be very nice Missus Watts. I'm sure he'd like that. Thank you."

"No trouble at all. I miss having a dog around the house. Don't you Alec?"

Alex smiled and rolled his eyes at them. "Yes, dear."

"Mister Apeman?" Cass said. "Would you mind giving me a hand for a moment? He looks like he might be a bit of a handful."

He hesitated, but nodded, and he and the dog followed her down-stairs, Cass cooing, "Come on Diogenes … good dog … come on little fella … good boy."

"Who's for a beer?" Alex asked the remaining three. "Anybody hungry?"

The quartet sat at a table on the patio in the shade of an awning with a warm breeze gently stirring the salty air and noshed on bowls of assorted nuts and drank ice cold Stella Artois, taking it in their turn to sigh.

"Fuckin' A, man," said Dude. "This is pretty nice."

Downstairs in the utility room, Cass attached a wall-secured halter around Little Diogenes' shoulders and turned on the water, running it until it was a comfortably warm temperature. Apeman watched as she liberally squirted shampoo over him and began to knead it into his fur. The dog stood patiently and let her. And when she suggested he lie down and roll over he did as she bid and agreeably laid there, his little back leg kicking, as she squirted more shampoo onto his stomach, and worked it thoroughly around the inside of his back legs and into the pink of his belly. Soon he looked like something Charlie Brown might be able to identify wafting above in the sky.

"Could you rinse him off Mister Apeman?" she said, handing him the nozzle. "I need to go get something."

Apeman finished the job while, unbeknownst to him, she retrieved a complete change of clothes from Alex's closet and laid them out on the bed of a downstairs guest bedroom. When she returned, The Pisser was absolutely drenched, as she'd suspected he would be, and Little Diogenes was struggling at his restraints.

"Oh my god, you're soaked!" she exclaimed in apparent surprise, displaying her several years of long-ago experience as a London stage actress.

She took up a large towel and engulfed the dog in it.

"I've got him," she said. "Why don't I finish this? Next door you'll find a change of clothes on the bed. There are towels and soap and sham-poo in the ensuite too. Even a fresh toothbrush and some Listerine if you like. Just leave your wet clothes in the hamper and I'll wash them for you."

The Pisser did as he was told.

Meanwhile Cass used Shakey's old flea comb and removed the corpses of dozens of dead fleas the size of grains of wild rice out of Little Diogenes' fur, then rubbed some left-over vet-prescribed flea treatment into the skin at the nape of his neck. The little terrier's tail wagged his appreciation and he seemed to almost purr with pleasure.

Upstairs Alex was trying to learn what he could about The Pisser. What was his origin story? How on Earth had he come to evolve in this way? What was his actual name?

No one knew. No one had even guessed before that day that he was American.

"He's clearly educated," said Alex. "Any idea what he studied at school, or what he did for work?"

"Work?" asked John sceptically.

"Dude? Do you have any ideas?"

"I have some theories, man. One or two hypotheses."

"Such as?"

"I think he did time. Like, a lot of time. Time enough to read a lot of books in the prison library. You should get him going on Greek philosophy. He'll go on for hours about the Stoics and all that Cynical School shit. I can see him alone in his cell reading about Diogenes pissing on people in the agora, flipping the bird at Plato, and insulting Alexander the Great. Cheering himself up vicariously, thrilling to his ancient misanthropy."

"Good lord. Prison? Do you know something, or are you merely guessing?"

"Just deducing, man. Just deducing. But it fits doesn't it? He doesn't have any books. I've never seen him with one anyway. You can't exactly lug a library around in a shopping cart. And yet he spends his days provoking anyone he comes across into debating everything from these obscure philosophical doctrines to macro-economics to climatology. The knowledge had to come from somewhere."

"If he was a draft dodger maybe he did time for burning his draft card," suggested Rog. "Maybe he got busted at a protest."

"Perhaps," Alex allowed. "But surely the simplest answer is that he's a former college philosophy teacher."

"Maybe. But he doesn't strike me as the kinda dude who could handle the discipline of a regimented education, man. Can you see him taking any sort of instruction? And if he'd been a college professor, wouldn't he have some sort of income? A pension? I mean, once you're on the tenure track you're set for life."

"To get on the tenure track you have to conform to a syllabus and a dress code and some sort of normative behaviour," said John. "Can you picture Ape doing any of those things?"

They all agreed this was highly unlikely.

"What does he say when you ask him?" said Alex.

They looked at each other, shrugging. Dude opened his mouth as though about to say something, then changed his mind and said nothing, looking perplexed.

"You've never enquired?" said Alex.

They shook their heads.

"Aren't you curious?"

They nodded their acknowledgement that they were.

"Well?"

"He is what he is," said Dude. "A man who's right for his time and place."

"The Stranger. Good one Dude," Rog said, congratulating him on the apt Lebowski reference. "He fits right in there," he added, citing another.

"'And even if he's a lazy man,'" contributed John, "' - and the Ape was most certainly that. Quite possibly the laziest in White Rock City, which would place him high in the runnin' for laziest worldwide. But sometimes there's a man, sometimes there's a man.'"

Alex laughed. "You're going to recite the entire script aren't you?"

"We could," answered Rog. "We've done it before."

"Often," said John.

Just then Little Diogenes hurtled up the stairs, hared through the house to the deck and, at the second attempt, vaulted onto Alex's lap to cries of "Look at you!" and "Who's that dog?" and "Who's a good boy then?"

Cass joined them, beaming.

"Not bad eh? He was so good. He just sat patiently while we washed him. And oh, how he loved the blowdryer. I thought he was going to ask for a cigarette afterward."

"If not for the eyes I'd think it was an entirely different dog," said Alex.

"I was going to mention that. I think we should ask Mister … What is his real name? I can't call somebody Apeman, it's demeaning."

"It's the only thing he answers to," said John. "Has been as long as I've known him."

Dude, Rog, and Alex nodded in agreement.

"Well I can't. It's self-hating. I'm going to find out his real name, or re-christen him myself."

Alex smiled and shrugged helplessly at them. "What can I say lads? She's Church of England. You know how believers can't help but drag Christ into everything."

She clapped him playfully over the head.

"Anyway, I think we should pay for little Diogenes to have Dr. White look at his eyes. What do you think?"

"Absolutely. Apeman won't object I'm sure. He claims he isn't his dog anyway."

"Good. It's decided then. Now, is this all you're offering them for lunch Epicurus? Nuts and beer?"

"I wasn't sure what you had planned, and Ape - he who shall be re-named - was otherwise engaged. So I thought we'd drink some beers and munch on these delicious mixed nuts until it was decided. Anyway, we have work to get down to. We have some hymns to write. Isn't that right lads?"

"Hymns?"

He nodded.

"You're writing hymns now? The man who sang, "'Slip Off Yer Panties'?"

He grinned at her.

"I can't wait to hear them. But why are you writing hymns suddenly? Are you boys Christian rockers or something?"

"No, Dude here is an ordained minster in the Church of the …. What is it again?"

"Latter Day Dude," said Dude.

"Latter Day Dude," echoed Alex. "And he assures me that mankind can be saved from extinction and the planet made safe for habitation if we can only come up with some catchy hymns that will convert the whole of creation to Dudeism's cause. So I agreed to try. It seems a worthy project, after all."

"I couldn't agree more. But first you'll be needing some lunch. You can't save the world on macadamia nuts and beer. What'll it be? Chicken? Egg salad? Tuna? Bacon and tomato? Is there anything that isn't kosher Mister Dude?"

"No, it's all good as far as The Dude is concerned. Eat what you like. To each his own, man."

"Sounds like a sensible religion. I'm sure it'll catch on. And you," she said, reaching out and scratching Little Diogenes' chin where he laid contentedly on Alex's lap, "shall have some Fancy Fare. I think we still have some tins left over. Come on," she turned and went to the kitchen with Little Diogenes trotting happily behind her.

"You're a lucky man," said John.

"We're all lucky merely to be alive at all," said Alex. "But I am luckier than most, I'll grant you."

All at once Dude abruptly stood up and uttered a "Je-sus," at the sight of Apeman. They all turned and gaped at him in wonder. He was wearing a pair of khaki trousers, an aquamarine golf shirt, a new pair of sandals, and was washed and combed and sweet-smelling. But for the beard, they would've seen his half dozen remaining teeth were minty fresh too.

"Look who's been resurrected!" Dude said, laughing.

"Whoa, Dapper Dan!" exclaimed John. "It's George Fucking Clooney."

"More like Willem Fucking Dafoe, isn't he?" said Rog.

"My word," said Alex. "What a transformation. What a metamorphosis."

Cass and Little Diogenes emerged onto the deck behind him. The dog sniffed at The Pisser's ankles and licked his foot in seeming approval.

"Well, well," said Cass. "Don't you look nice. You're just in time for lunch Mister, Mister … I'm not calling you Apeman. I'm sorry. I can't do it."

She considered it for a moment and decided, "I shall christen you … Manus. You are no longer Ape. You have evolved. You are a man, and you are one of us. Man-us. Et voila."

"Very on the nose, Dear. No doubt the Earl of Oxford's reasoning when writing Timon of Athens."

"Hmm? Oh yes, of course. Shakespeare. Apemantus. I hadn't thought of that. I never played Timon, so I've never actually read it. Alls Well and Much Ado, however, I've read. I suppose I should suggest we call him King of France or Dogberry instead."

"I think Manus will do."

"Mister Manus, what will you have? Is chicken salad, alright?"

"Thank you," he said.

"Chicken salad it is, Mister Manus." She returned inside.

"Manus," considered Alex. "I like it. It suits you."

"This act of appellation will stand," paraphrased John in his best Bush the Elder voice, to appreciative murmurs of "nice one" from Dude and Rog.

"Manus," said Alex, standing, "have a seat there. Can I get you a beer? Or would you care for a glass of wine? We've got some very good reds. A nice Cab Franc or a Malbec? We've also got some very decent Syrahs if you prefer. Or whites, we have some good whites too for a hot late spring day. Whatever you like."

"Water will be fine, thank you."

"You're sure? I can't convince you to take a glass of Shiraz? Because I'd love an excuse to open a bottle."

"If you insist."

"There we are!" Alex nearly shouted. "We've turned a water into wine!"

He patted Manus firmly on the shoulder as he walked past him into the house, saying, "Excellent, excellent."

He returned with a bottle and a tray of glasses.

"We really must drink a toast to Dude's completed vax status."

He filled the glasses and passed them round.

"To freedom from disease, to essential workers everywhere, and to those who've sadly gone before."

"Hear, hear," they all affirmed and drank.

"Glad to see you drinking a toast to the vaccine John," said Alex. "I was afraid you actually meant all that anti-vax nonsense."

"Hey, don't read too much into it. I'll drink to anything if there's quality booze involved. Even a Big Government/Big Pharma conspiracy to reduce population."

"John, you seem a sensible enough fellow otherwise. How can you possibly believe all that insane rubbish?"

"Oh man," Dude sotto voce'd, "don't get him started."

"I just don't think it's right for the government to tell me what to put in my body."

"There are millions dead, many millions more with terrible lingering effects. What more important purpose could there be for governments than to administer crucial public health measures during a global pandemic?"

"It's just a fuckin' hoax. I had it, it was a big nothing. A bit of flu. That's all."

"Well good for you. But you can still be a carrier and pass it on to others, even if it doesn't make you sick.

You see, that's the kind of attitude I don't understand. They talk about money or religion being the root of all evil, but that kind of selfishness, that 'I'm alright Jackism', if it isn't the root of all evil it has to be a significant rhizome of it."

"It's not about selfishness. It's about freedom: my freedom to …"

"Get sick and die?"

"Why not? If I want to take the risk of getting sick and maybe dying, that's my business not their's."

"It is their's. And it's the business of everyone who comes within six feet of you too. Or within six feet of anyone else who has come into contact with you. Or within six feet of someone who came into contact with someone who knows someone who knows someone who came within six feet of you. On and on and on like looking into a mirror endlessly reflecting itself into eternity. Just because you choose to risk those odds, doesn't mean everyone else should have to chance it.

And as far as the government goes, they have a perfect right to tell us what we may or may not choose to risk. You're inoculated against measles aren't you? And TB? And polio? We're prohibited from driving drunk. We have speed limits and seat belts and environmental laws and financial regulations and consumer protections and so on. It is the very business of government in organized societies to set limits on freedoms. Otherwise it'd all be just anarchy and dystopia."

"For a lot of people it's already anarchy and dystopia," said Manus. "The anarchic freedom of the richest few to skirt any laws and evade any taxes or restraints society might try to impose on them for the greater good of the many; and the dystopia suffered by the growing multitudes who are left defenceless against the consequences. If you were poor you too might smile at the thought of some anarchy reaching the walled-off estates of the monied classes. Why not give the fat cats a taste of our dystopian reality? Unlike them, we're freely willing to share."

"Really?" Alex said in answer to The Pisser, then turned and asked John, "Is that true John? You and the rest of the anti-vaxxer crowd are content to risk your own health and the health of everybody else as an act of rebellion against the fact Jeff Bezos and Elon Musk refuse to pay their fair share of taxes?

Well, if that's the reasoning I stand corrected. Here I thought it was just ignorant, paranoid, superstitious, chickenshit needle-phobia, when in fact you anti-vaxxers are all modern day freedom fighters acting on principle, selflessly sacrificing your own fates and the fates of others to call attention to the fact that Jeff Bezos and Elon Musk are greedy cunts who should pay more tax. In that case, I salute you. Bravo."

He stood. "I'll just go see how Cass is getting on with the lunch shall I?"

"Ape, calm down man," said Dude pointedly when Alex was out of earshot.

"I am calm," he said.

"Calmer than Alex," said John.

"They're nice people. There's no reason to insult them. It's very un-Dude."

"I wasn't being insulting," said Ape. "I was just pointing out in a general way that people who shield themselves behind walls and gates are, ipso facto, partitioning themselves off from society, hiding in effect from the consequences of the gross inequality that is exemplified by those very walls and gates. 'I'm alright Jack-ism,' he says. Well, if the mansion fits, I say."

"Yeah whatever, but there's still no reason to be rude."

"I don't think it is rude to point out what is plainly evident. They are obscenely rich, and we are not. I'm sure they've noticed that too."

Alex and Cass returned to the patio with a large silver tray bearing an array of sandwiches of various types, side plates, cloth napkins, and another bottle of wine. Little Diogenes followed, licking the last traces of Fancy Fare Steak and Kidney from his muzzle.

"Here we are," announced Cass, to exclamations of: Man that looks good. Yum yum. I could tuck into that, etcetera.

"Very nice," said Manus, while Alex topped up his glass. He cast a meaningful glance Dude's way.

"We should drink a toast."

They raised their glasses, Dude doing so with some trepidation.

"From all of us, and on behalf of Diogenes too of course, we thank you for your hospitality."

They all drank. Dude exhaled with relief and drank too, just as The Pisser added, "This is such a beautiful home …"

An urgent need to be stifling whatever provocative thing was about to come out of Ape's mouth coincided with Dude's attempt to swallow his wine.

"How many square feet is it?" Manus enquired over Dude's sudden convulsive coughing.

"A little under six thousand," Alex said.

"And it's just the two of you living here?"

Dude, who had recovered and was about to chance another sip of wine, lowered his glass without drinking and pushed it away.

"It used to be five," said Cass. "But the kids have all flown the nest now."

Apeman nodded equably.

"Our daughter studies drama in New York, we have one boy studying music at Oxford, like his dad, and our other son is a session player in Los Angeles."

"That's nice. I guess you haven't seen them for a while."

"No, it's been terrible. They're like homing pigeons usually. We're constantly having to drive out to the airport to pick one or the other of them up. So this last year and a half has been almost unbearable."

"For us more than them, no doubt," said Alex.

"Well, quite," agreed Cass, laughing.

"They couldn't get into colleges closer to home?" The Pisser asked placidly.

"Not of the calibre of Oxford and Juilliard, no."

"Oh right. Of course not. Stupid of me. It's the prerogative of the rich to perpetuate their endless advantages."

"I don't know if prerogative is quite the way I'd put it. It's not really a 'right' or a 'privilege' in that sense. More like an affordable investment to better serve our children's futures," said Alex.

"Which is kind of in the job description for parents I think," added Cass. "Do you have kids Mister Manus?"

"No, thank god. Can't abide them. Noisy, troublesome little brutes. Yours excepted, I'm sure."

"Don't be," Alex said. "They were plenty noisy and troublesome to us when they were young."

"And now they merely trouble all of humanity with their selfish contribution of greenhouse gasses to an already poisoned atmosphere."

"Those planes would've flown whether they were on them or not," said Alex, irked.

"Maybe. But not if enough other people of conscience chose not to blithely add more jet fuel to the fire. Airlines won't fly empty planes forever. Not if governments are forced finally to balk at having to continually bail them out."

"And if we let the airlines fail? What then? How do we travel?" asked Cass.

"We travelled the planet in sailing ships for hundreds of years. Thousands of years. We could go back to that. The technology is infinitely better now."

"Yes, but it would still take days to get to Europe or anywhere else," said Alex. "If you wanted to go to Hawaii for your vacation you'd spend almost your entire holiday merely sailing there. It would kill tourism. What happens to all those millions of jobs?"

"I dunno, a week or so sailing to and from Hawaii or Europe sounds like a pretty nice holiday to me," said Rog.

"And if you're prone to seasickness?" said Cass.

"Well then you could try vacationing closer to home," returned Apeman. "Maybe learn to appreciate your own surroundings, tour your own region in your electric car or by rail.

And as for the jobs, they'd still be there. Just different ones. And probably more of them. There is so much work to be done remaking our entire economy and way of life. There'll be more jobs that need doing than people to do them.

And anyway, where'd we get the idea that we're all entitled to get everything we want as soon as we want it anyway? Who sped up time like this? It's an affront to nature. When did we decide this was a good idea? If you want to go from one side of the planet to the other you should have to put in the effort and invest the time. It's no small thing to travel thousands of miles. It's not something you should be able to do and still get home in time for dinner.

Maybe if we were forced to stop treating the world like it was an obstacle to be avoided by flying over, an inconvenient annoyance between Point A and Point B, then we'd take better care of it. They talk about the harm the neglect of fly-over states in America has wrought, well, the whole world has become a fly-over state. Something lying thirty thousand feet below, obscured by clouds. How do we care for something we never see and never experience? We've lost touch with the earth. We need to get grounded."

"We gotta get back to the garden," said Dude, channeling Joni Mitchell.

"When we want books or toilet paper or godknowswhat, we're too lazy or selfish or witless to walk down to a local shop and buy it. We don't think of maybe supporting a local business and employing a fellow human being. No. We want it right now. ASAP. So we send our money, or take on debt, and feed it to that ultimate super hero movie villain made manifest, Jeff Bezos. A little circumcised dick of a man who somehow bestrides the planet like a Colossus.

No wonder so many rubes are so willing to buy all these bullshit online conspiracy theories. They're no more bizarre than the reality we're living. We are, most of us, actively colluding with a few billionaires and their political and corporate henchmen to systematically destroy ourselves and the civilization we've built over thousands of years. All so that a few obscenely rich people can grow even more grotesquely wealthy for no fathomable reason whatever that I can see. How do you top that for batshit lunacy?

The heads of the fossil fuel companies, and bankers and hedge fund managers, and the Republican party in America, and Rupert Murdoch, and Mark Zuckerberg, and Peter Thiel, and whichever Koch brother is still breathing, and all the other fascists and dictators around the world, and anyone else for that matter, who has aided and abetted this systematic attempt at global genocide, should be standing in the dock Nuremberg-style, on trial for crimes against all humanity. That would be a rational response to reality."

"That's a fine soliloquy. But have you got a solution for any of this?" asked Alex. "Or are you just Macbeth cursing the candles for lighting fools on their way to dusty death? Never mind our yesterdays, or our tomorrows for that matter. What do you propose we do today?"

"Well, first of all, we could outlaw billionaires."

"How do we go about doing that, pray tell?"

"Simple. Shut down all tax havens, worldwide. At the point of a gun, or many guns, or large artillery, if necessary. Then tax all personal assets and estates worth over a billion dollars at one hundred percent. Pour those trillions of dollars into climate mitigation efforts, green technology investments, healthcare and education funding, and scientific research into advanced farming techniques.

Nationalize all fossil fuel corporations and seize their assets for the benefit of ordinary citizens and climate mitigation efforts. Then ban all investment in fossil fuel exploration, outlaw any investment in fossil fuel infrastructure - and not just pipelines, but gas stations and airports, and in residential and commercial construction. Set a stop date at which we are forbidden to produce or burn any more fossil fuels. 2030 would be a target year that might give us a fighting chance of survival.

Ban all fossil-fuel powered vehicles. Ground all nonessential air travel. Shut down all national militaries and airforces and allow only United Nations peacekeeping forces to resolve conflicts and to aide the billions of climate refugees we're going to be creating.

I could go on and on. The list is as endless as all the recovered hoarded loot would be. That would make a good start I should think."

Manus paused and waited for a rebuttal.

The response of the table to his suggestions was silence. But a thoughtful silence rather than the embarrassed silences John's diatribes usually engendered. After all, who could argue with his thesis? The Pisser simply gave voice to what was plainly evident. A climate catastrophe was hoving into view like a waterfall on a river and we were collectively, madly, paddling toward it like we were in a tearing hurry to plunge over the edge.

"You know, the whole public fascination with billionaires is a recent phenomena," Manus continued. "When I was a kid there was Howard Hughes and J Paul Getty and maybe a handful of others we couldn't name. Before that there was John D Rockefeller and maybe one or two others worth the equivalent amount to a billion at the time.

These people were despised. Why do we celebrate these assholes now? They should be deeply ashamed of themselves. And if they haven't the conscience or self-awareness or the plain decency to be ashamed of themselves voluntarily, we should beleaguer them with such inexhaustible vitriolic abuse that they are made to see how immoral their selfish behaviour is. These people are sick, mentally deranged, homicidal. They are psychopaths. And they should be shunned, vilified, clapped in irons if need be, to stop them from turning this planet into a barren, uninhabitable rock in order to satisfy their pathological cupidity."

Off in the distance to the southeast came the distant blast of a train whistle. Diogenes, lying at Cass's feet next to the table, lifted his head toward the noise.

"Well we haven't been travelling anywhere further than the grocery store for a year and a half. And until the pandemic we hardly used Amazon, so I guess in our own small way we're trying to do our part," said Cass.

"Aha! See? Amazon," said John. "You said it yourself. Follow the money. Whose government lab produced the virus? China's. Who profited the most from the pandemic? Jeff Bezos. Who does more business with China than Jeff Bezos? No one."

This elicited the aforementioned embarrassed silence.

"And we have solar panels on the roof," continued Alex, ignoring John. "And we drive electric cars. And we recycle. And we've mostly given up eating beef."

"That's very commendable. I wasn't accusing you. You're clearly two of the virtuous ones, doing more than most," said Manus, possibly sarcastically.

"Well, returning to where this conversation began, giving our kids fewer opportunities in life, or seeing them less often, or giving up our too-large home of thirty years isn't going to make any difference in the fight against climate change," said Cass. "And personal habits have little to do with it anyway. I read in The Guardian that just a few corporations are responsible for most of the emissions. So making yourself unhappy purely on a point of principle isn't going to do anybody any good, is it?"

"Well, that's debatable. Every little bit helps. At the very least it couldn't hurt. And the pleasures of righteousness are vastly under-rated."

"Well, that's just like, your opinion man," said Alex.

The whistle's long lonely peal of warning grew nearer in concert with the rumble of the approaching freight.

"Is it twelve o'clock already?" asked Alex. Cass nodded. "Blimey."

The whistle was growing louder now. The rumbling more disturbing. The plates on the table began to rattle just perceptively and little ripples of perturbation appeared in their wine glasses. Little Diogenes yipped a brief uncertain bark of alarm in its general direction. Nevertheless, it persisted, getting louder until it seemed the house began to shake on its foundation.

"If we're going to get something done today we'd better get down to the studio," Alex shouted.

Little Diogenes was standing now, fully alert, hackles raised, barking for all his life. Cass reached down to calm him, to little avail.

On and on the deafening thunder roared, punctuated at intervals by the whistle. They fell silent in the din patiently measuring out the passing time, having a sip of wine, dabbing at the corner of a mouth with a napkin, moving the stem of a wine glass a millimetre to the left, idly watching the progress of a far off yacht. At length the tremors and racket subsided enough for them to be able to hear the dog's low agitated growling, and their conversation could continue.

"Long one today," said Alex.

"What is there, like, four coal trains a day now?" asked Rog. "I thought we were going to ban coal exports."

"Hardly. They've stepped them up since Trump, I think," said Alex. "I think it's more like six a day. And they invested tens of millions enlarging the coal terminal too, so I guess they mean to keep running them flat-out for the foreseeable. Old white guys in Congress keep their jobs ensuring they keep digging up the stuff, even if it's too dirty even for American ports to want to touch it. So we're stuck with it I guess. Jobs jobs jobs, goes the mantra."

Apeman was about to say something when Alex abruptly got up and announced it was time to get down to work.

***

In the basement was a large room, once a home theatre, now converted into a recording studio. Tapestries hung from the walls, and Persian rugs covered the tile floor, really tying the room together, but also with the added benefit of deadening echo. A gleaming black Steinway grand piano stood at the centre of the room, flanked by multiple keyboards. Racks of dozens of guitars lined one entire wall. Mic stands, amplifiers, a drum kit, and various other percussion instruments, bongos, maracas, and tambourines filled the space. At one end was a window into what had once been a wine-tasting room, but was now a control booth containing a mixing board.

Dude, John, and Rog stood and gaped in wonder at the sight of it all.

"This is fucking awesome," said John at last.

"Do you play?" Alex asked him.

"Me? No."

"Any of you play? Dude?"

"No man. I played the xylophone at our grade 3 Christmas concert. That's about it."

"So none of you play an instrument?"

"We played the recorder and the banjo in Miss Caplan's class Dude," said Rog.

"Oh yeah. Miss Caplan," he replied wistfully. "I'd forgotten about her."

"You forgot about Miss Caplan?" John said, astounded. "Jesus Dude. That kind of forgetfulness should worry you. Miss Caplan?! I got my first boner over that woman. My first few hundred probably. She should be like Pavlov's Dog's dinner bell. Just hearing her name should not only make you drool, you should get a stiffy. Dude, I hate to say it, but you have officially smoked too much weed."

"Yeah, well, you know John, that was a long time ago. We're getting older. The only stiffy that concerns me now is whether or not my turds are hard."

Alex took this exchange as a no, and wandered away and sat at the Steinway. He took a sip of wine and rested the glass on a coaster on top of the piano and absentmindedly plunked out a C minor triad.

"We should probably start with a little Bach," he announced, beginning to play Jesu, Joy of Man's Desiring. "This might be suitable for purpose."

"Oh, I know this," said Dude. "We're gonna write lyrics to this?"

"I thought we might. If you're going to steal, steal from the best I always say. Rog," he said, "what was that doggerel you were saying earlier?"

"Doggerel?"

"That crude verse you were spouting about Dude."

"Oh, right."

He looked at the ceiling tiles and tried to remember.

"Something about weed is the way and the word?" Alex prompted.

"Right, right. I remember I think. 'Weed is the word, and the word is the way, we follow Dude's example, tho we used to call him Ray.'"

"Hmm." Alex considered this for a moment. "Not sure that's going to work with the melody. We'll have to try something else."

He turned round on the bench, away from the piano, and addressed a Hammond organ, on which he began to play some chords that started out as Bach's Toccata and Fugue in D minor, but then drifted into Chest Fever, before morphing into something approximating In A Gadda Da Vida.

"Weedistheword …and ..the ..word .. is .. the ..way …" he sang.

He played the chords again, and repeated the phrase. And then he played it again, and then again, humming the lyrics now rather than singing them as though he were tired of them already. Doodoodoodoo …doo doo doo doo.

"Mind if I do a J?" asked Dude.

"Not at all," Alex replied, distracted. "It can only help."

They all shared a joint while Alex noodled on the keyboards. When the doobie was done Alex suggested they get a vocal track down. He told Rog to stand at a mic while he went into the booth. When he emerged he instructed him to sing the lines into the mic.

"You're going to record this?" he asked, alarmed.

"We're recording right now. We're rolling tape man. Just speak the lines into the mic as you did before, and then repeat it in a slightly different way. Different tempo, different phrasing. Start slow and increase the pace as you get more confident. Just relax into it. Eventually you'll find yourself singing and we'll get a useable take. Then I'll write some music around it. Lay down a piano and organ pad. Add a string swell. Then we'll try and come up with a couple more verses and we'll work up a choral backing by multi-tracking our voices. That should drown your vocal out effectively enough."

"This is fucking cool," John said. "Is this digital or are you old school tape?"

"Decidedly old school, John. We roll tape here."

After several minutes Rog had exhausted new ways of phrasing the few lyrics they had and was beginning to get into a rock star vibe, holding the mic in both hands and passionately mimicking an over-enthusiastic karaoke singer, "Hey Dude, don't make it bad ..."

Alex laughed. "Oh that is good. Hey Dude!"

He started singing quietly, "Hey Dude ..." while playing it softly on the piano. Then louder, singing, "Hey Dude ..." heavier on the keys, "Hey Dude, don't be a something ... we need a lyric here. Hey Dude, don't be a berk ..."

"Nanana na na na na," nanaed John unhelpfully.

"Yeah, we'll get to that," said Alex. "We need some actual lyrics first. We'll take the nana's as written."

"Hey Dude, don't be a saint ..." sang Dude, trancelike, while the others hummed along.

John flashed Dude a gleeful 'Can-you-believe-it-we're-singing-Hey-Jude-with-Alex-fucking-Watts' look.

Dude beamed at him serenely as though this miracle was all part of some divinely inspired plan that he alone was privy to.

And yes, it was pretty fucking cool too.

****

Meanwhile, upstairs on the patio, Cass returned from the kitchen having cleared the lunch detritus away, to find Apeman still sitting at the table considering the view.

"Ah, Mister Manus, not making music with the others then?"

"No," he replied dismissively, as though the very thought of making music was beneath his dignity.

"You don't approve of music?" He said nothing. "Or is it pleasure itself that you have a problem with?"

"I enjoy the pleasures freely provided by the Earth. The sun, a cooling breeze, a beautiful wide view of the sea, as you enjoy here," he said, nodding toward the ocean.

"Well surely music is a pleasure freely provided by the Earth isn't it?"

He considered this for a moment, frowning.

"I don't think so," he said at last. "Guitars and pianos and microphones and tape machines didn't evolve from the primordial stew of creation."

"No, but music is just waves of sound arranged in a pleasant tonal order for the benefit of any receptive ears that may happen to be around to catch them, isn't it? And if I'm not mistaken, these vibrations are really just waves of energy. I have no training in physics or what-have-you, but I think that may be right.

And isn't the entire universe powered by waves of energy emitting outward from the original Big Bang? Like time itself in fact? Moving forward through space? And what could be more natural and freely given than enjoying the remnants of the ultimate creation story: The Big Bang? Like Joni Mitchell sang, we're all just stardust, Mister Manus, and music is the breath of the universe."

"If that accurately described music I would agree with you. Have you heard any lately? It's nowt but noise as you English would say."

"Hmm, well. We English have another saying, 'Taking the piss.' And I believe you're taking the piss with me Mister Manus. You're having me on. You don't mean a word of this. Or much else of what you say I'd wager. You're just a sour, wounded old contrarian aren't you? Spoiling for an argument to amuse yourself and ease your boredom. Well I'm not buying it. Nobody hates music. Not even Hitler hated music. He was into Wagner."

"Do you think Donald Trump thrills to the Euterpean muse?"

She laughed. "Ooh, I like that. Euterpean muse. She was the - I'm assuming it was a she, right? - the muse of music?"

"The Greek god of music and lyric poetry."

"Euterpean muse. How lovely. I must tell Alec. I wonder if he knows. It'd make a fine album title."

She rose and went inside, retrieved a pen and paper and returned.

"How do you spell that?"

Apeman spelled it out for her.

When this was accomplished she continued, "What were we saying? Oh yes, Donald Trump. No, he's undoubtedly an exception to the rule. But saying that preposterous cretin is in favour of anything is a sure sign that that something must be evil."

She paused, filling their glasses with the last of the bottle.

"This is the product of the Dionysian muse Mister Manus - I do know that one."

She raised her glass in salute to the muse of the grape.

"Now then Mister Manus, I don't understand this pose of your's, this angry, mad at the world, disdainful of pleasure act. I don't believe it for a minute. Or I don't understand it anyway.

I agree with your assessment of the climate crisis. I agree wholeheartedly that we're all not doing enough. Ourselves included. I fully understand your urgency on the environment and your stridency about economic inequality. I do. And if it will help for me to sit on a street corner wearing a placard stating that the end is nigh and the rich should be eaten, I will.

But at the end of the day you have to try to put it behind you. At least for a time. This is the only life you're going to get. Don't waste all of it miserably haranguing people. Treat your activism as a job. Devote eight hours a day to saving the world and the rest to taking pleasure from it and enjoying the immense good fortune we all share at being alive at all. Gather ye rosebuds while ye may, Mister Manus."

"I'm hardly a virginal girl, Missus Watts. But I take your meaning."

He tilted his glass toward her and drank.

"You must call me Cass, Mister Manus."

"And you may call me Caleb," he burped.

"Caleb? That's nice. Caleb what?"

"Caleb van Buskirk."

"What a lovely name! Caleb, may I ask … Alec tells me you're … out of doors, is the way he put it. Is that right?"

"Yes."

"I see. How does that work? If you don't mind me asking. Do you have a set spot where you bed down at night? Some place where you keep your belongings? Or do you move around a lot?"

"I keep some things at the shelter on Foster Street. When the weather is really bad I often stay there. But mostly Diogenes and I pitch a tent in Olympic View Park. No one bothers us much."

"You know, we do have a lot of room here. There's an entire self-contained suite over the garage. You could come and go as you please. There's a nice little kitchen so you could cook for yourself. Or if you'd like, you could eat with us. It'd be no trouble. And you said yourself that we have so much. You'd be perfectly safe here and have all the privacy you need."

"It's nice of you to offer. Really. But it's miles from anywhere out here. I go to The Marketplace every day. It's kind of like my ministry, where I go to … well, as you said, miserably harangue people about global warming. And I'm too old to walk all the way to Uptown and back from here. It just wouldn't be convenient."

"There's the bus. It goes by regularly. We could get you a pass. Or a car. We could find you a serviceable car for transportation. Do you have a license?"

"Not anymore, no. I used to have a camper van. But the city clamped down on poor people living in motorhomes on the street and towed it one day when I was out. I couldn't afford to bail it out of the wrecking yard. After that a driver's license seemed surplus to my requirements, so I let it lapse."

"Well, Alec drives to Uptown every day to take his walk. There are sidewalks there, and the ground is much less hilly than around here. He could drive you. And I drive to The Marketplace practically every day to do the shopping too, so you could ride with me as well."

"I'll think about it," he lied.

"I hope you will. Truly."

"How often do those coal trains go past?" he asked, changing the subject.

"Oh, I don't know, I've stopped counting. Far more often than they used to do, that's for sure. Four a day? Possibly more. Six maybe? I hardly even notice them anymore. Alex sleeps right through them now they're so regular. And then there's the Amtrak. Two of those every day as well. But you get used to it. We're English. We love trains."

"Funny how that works isn't it? It's like something akin to nominative determinism. Only instead of your name somehow determining your choice of career, your ancestry somehow passes down through the generations a preference for this, that, or the other thing from an old country you never lived in. My family are Dutch. We all have a special affinity for tulips."

"Caleb van Buskirk! You're a tulip fancier? So am I! I have dozens of varieties."

"I noticed," he said.

"They're so beautiful, aren't they? So warm and colourful. So charming."

"'How can you be content to be in the world like tulips in the garden, to make a fine show, and be good for nothing,'" quoted The Pisser. "My admiration for tulips is less aesthetic than it is practical. If not for tulip bulbs, my family would never have survived the war."

"Your family ate them?"

He nodded.

"Oh dear. I've read about that. I do love tulips, but the thought of eating them is ghastly. But on the other hand, it means they were good for something, weren't they?"

"Yes. And I remind myself to think about that fact a lot. It gives me a useful perspective on my own life. As difficult as things may get for me, it's as nothing compared to what my parents and their families suffered. By comparison I have it pretty easy. So far at least."

"That's very wise Caleb. You're full of surprises aren't you? Your erudition, your eloquence …"

"Not what you'd expect from a bum?"

"That's not what I meant."

"Sure it is. It's okay. There's no point in not calling a thing what it is."

"You are not a thing either."

"No, you're right, I'm not. I am a man. I am a conscientious objector. And I am unused to wine and late for the bathroom."

He stood, a little unsteadily.

"Which way?" he asked.

"Through the kitchen, take a left at the fridge, at the end of the hall."

"Thank you," he said over his shoulder, hastily reeling through the doors only just eluding Alex coming in the opposite direction.

"'Drink for the Apeman' …" he sang in possibly the most obscure musical reference ever uttered.

Cass looked at him quizzically.

"Clap for the Wolfman," he explained. "The Guess Who."

"I don't know. I don't recognize it. Who?"

"No, the band. The band is The Guess Who."

"Oh, I see. How's it coming with you and your band?"

"Brilliant. We're ready for you."

"Ready for me? Whatever for?"

"You and Apemantus. We've written some lyrics. There's a chorus. We need some back-up singers."

"Sounds lovely."

He bent down and kissed her. Little Diogenes, dozing at her feet, roused himself to nudge his shin with his chin. Alex reached down and scratched him.

"Hello Little Diogenes. How's Big Diogenes doing?" he enquired of Cass. "Have you got him drunk yet?"

"I believe so. And his name is Caleb. Caleb van Bush-something."

"Good heavens. Van Bushsomething? What an extraordinary name. Well, let's see if Mr. van Bushsomething will sing for his supper shall we?"

"Well you can ask him, but I don't think he'll be very keen. He's already got one you see."

Alex recognized the reference immediately.

"That's very good. John Cleese. The Frenchman. The Holy Grail. You're a remarkably erudite woman, you know that?"

He kissed her again.

"Remarkably erudite for a woman, you mean?"

"You know what I mean. For a human animal. I can't just say 'you're remarkably erudite for a human being' can I? That'd be absurd. Only humans can be erudite. Have you ever met a learned dog or ape?"

"Still, you have to be extra sensitive these days. You know how it is."

"Yes I do know how it is. And I'm getting mightily vexed by this nonsense. Every mundane conversation these days seems to get bogged down in pronoun trouble. You know what? Maybe we should just fuck all

51

the pronoun-identifying and gender fluidism and just stick to 'human be-ings' and be done with it. We're all fucking human beings. Can everybody be happy now for fuck sake?"

"I think that's rather the point love. Anyway, I'm always happy. And you seem happier than usual. You've been smoking cannabis haven't you?"

"I have. And in honour of the sacred herb I've re-purposed Hey Jude for the cause of promulgating the civilization-preserving properties of Dudeism."

"Good lord," said Cass. "You *are* going to save the world?"

He nodded solemnly.

"Well then, I'd better do my part."

In the studio Alex sat at the piano and Cass, Dude, John, and Rog made like The Supremes at a row of mic stands.

Little Diogenes was left whimpering outside the studio door, while Apeman, who had declined to sing for his supper, remained on the patio in a deep thinker's pose.

After a moment to adopt the proper devotional attitude, Alex began to play.

> Hey Dude, no breaking bad
> Take a zen song, and make it western
> Remember to take the truth of The Tao
> Then you allow, a wider spectrum
>
> Hey Dude, don't be a-fright
> Things look bad now,
> But new shit will come to light
> The minute you accept the ins and the outs
> Then you can shout, to take it easy
>
> And anytime you feel the pain, hey Dude, refrain
> The world is strikes and it is gutter balls
> For well you know that it's unDude to cop a 'tude
> There's always a chance you'll get some coitus
> Na na na na na nananana

Hey Dude, don't be afeared
There is yoga, and there are beverages here
Remember to take the ups and the downs
Lighten your mind, you'll keep it limber

So let it out and let it in, hey Dude, begin
You have to admit, that's once nice marmot
And don't you know Wu Wei may do a hit of a doob
Or take a wiz upon your carpet
Na na na na na nananana na na na na

Hey Dude, don't make it bad
The world is Walter, but it is Donny too
Remember to live the Tao of The Dude
No need to brood, just make it better
Better better better better better better Owwwwww
Yeah yeah yeah yeah yeah
Na na na nananana nananana hey Dude
Na na na nananana nananana hey Dude
Doo doo dee doo dee doody doody OW WOW!
Na na na nananana nananana hey Dude
Sing it Dude!

They continued with the chorus almost endlessly like the original until Alex called an end to Take 27.

"Cut. That's enough for a fade. Beautiful everybody. That one is a keeper."

When they were finished laughing, Cass suggested ordering in Chinese food and they returned to the patio, opened two more bottles of wine and toasted the setting sun. It had been an eventful day. A happy, creative, productive day. And it wasn't yet over.

*****

Alex sipped at his wine, bathed in the brilliance of the sun, and sighed in perfect contentment. On the horizon across a glittering sea was a golden yellow and blood red orb, looking like the top half of a ripe peach, sliding down the sky, gradually disappearing from view. Dude,

John, and Rog watched the show in similar silent smiling appreciation. Even Apeman seemed enraptured by it all.

"Ahhhh, Canadian sunset," Alex said. The others grinned and nodded.

Cass appeared with a large plate of scallops and bacon, and a platter of nachos and various dips and set them on the table.

"The Chinese will be here in forty-five minutes or so. I thought you might like these to tide you over til then."

Alex spryly rose to his feet and took her in his arms and began to dance her around, crooning,

"Once, I was alone, doodoo doo doo doo doo doo doodoo doo doo doo doo/ So, lonely and then/ You came, out of nowhere/ Like the sun, up from the hills/ Cold, cold was the wind/ Warm, warm were your lips/ Out there, on that ski trail, where your kiss, filled me with thrills/ A weekend in Canada/ a change of scene, was the most I bargained for/ And then I discovered you, and in your eyes/ I found that love, I couldn't ignore/ Down, down came the sun/ Fast, fast beat my heart/ I knew, when the sun set, from that day, we'd never part."

Finishing, he twirled her round, kissed her, and bowed gallantly as she took her seat, waving at her face as though with a fan and saying breathlessly, "I do declare, someone is mixing his Viagra and his wine again."

"Who needs Viagra on a night like this?" Alex scoffed. "'Such a night … it's such a night … sweet confusion under the moonlight …'"

"Doctor John, far out," said Dude, blowing on a scalding scallop. "Such a song."

Heads nodded in agreement, then bent to the task of eating. This they did, happily, greedily, wordlessly, until simple good manners dictated that each not be the one to scarf the last chip, blob of melted cheese, shallot, or bit of olive. When they were done they drank deeply, and with relish.

"You're looking very pleased with yourselves, I must say," said Cass. They grinned at her.

"And so we should," said Alex. "We made music today. And it is always perfect bliss to add to the music of the spheres."

"Good vibrations, man," said Dude.

"Well, perfect bliss it may be," she replied, "but some of those rhymes could be more harmonious."

"Some of the rhymes in the original weren't too clever either," said Alex.

"And they were the fuckin' Beatles," said John.

"Yeah," agreed Alex. "The fucking Beatles. So there, Missus Critic Lady."

"Are you going to overdub some backing to it?" she asked.

"I thought I might. I like the sound of it now. Simple piano. It has a kind of Psalmic quality I think. But then again, it does sort of cry out for some Ringo drum fills doesn't it?"

"I do, yes. And guitars and bass too. And then I think you should release it as a single."

"Get the fuck out," said John.

"I'm quite serious. It's amusing. And it has a kind of weird wisdom to it. The Dude speaks to people. There's a method to that madness."

"The Coen Brothers would sue," said Alex.

"Why do you say that? I think it might be something like what they intended. They didn't make The Big Lebowski simply to make people laugh. They could have done that with a story much less deep in subtext. They were trying to make people think. The Dude is an expression of idealism. It's a call for human beings to adapt the sacred texts of the past to form a belief system more suited to our present, evolved, self-destructive civilization."

"To add to the whole durned human comedy before it's too late to see ya further on down the trail, in the parlance of The Stranger," said Dude. "She's right, man. We should do it. Let's put it out there."

"A wiser feller than myself once said, fuckin' A," said John.

"Well, when you put it that way," said Alex. "Let's go make like Ringo."

"And George?" said Rog.

"We'll do all the Fabs," said Alex.

"There's just one thing," said Cass as they stood to leave.

"What's that?"

"Why does it have to be Hey Dude? Why not Hey Dudette?"

"What do you mean?"

"Well it just seems to me that if you're going to promote a faith to global religious primacy it ought to be fronted by a woman this time. I should think you men have had your innings. Just look at what you lot have wrought. Endless wars and inequality and ignorance and intolerance and now an existential environmental crisis.

We've had thousands of years of patriarchal faiths. This is our last chance to save life on Earth. Surely anything other than a universal matriarchal religion is the equivalent of doing the same thing over and over and expecting a different result. Maybe it's time humanity placed its faith in a Supreme Female Being."

"But The Dude is a dude," said Dude. "He's Jeff Lebowski, not Josephine Lebowski."

"But as I recall The Dude fathered a child with what's-her-name, that actress from Children of Men, and the one where she's a doctor that gets Alzheimer's."

"Julianne Moore," said Rog.

"Right. Julianne Moore. What if that child, the Christ Child in effect, was a girl? And The Dude and the other two …"

"Walter and Donnie," said Rog.

"… Walter and Donnie, thank you, were the three Magi?"

"Walter and Donnie and The Dude? The Three Wise Men?" said John.

"It's an intriguing idea," said Alex.

"No, it's not. It's absurd," replied John. "First of all, it's The Church of the Latter Day DUDE. Not The Church of the Latter Day Dudette. And second of all, Donnie was already dead before the Little Dude was born. That would leave Two Wise Men to praise him which is a lot less … um, praiseful. It doesn't work."

"It's true in terms of the meter too," admitted Alex. "It doesn't track. Hey Dudette? One syllable too many, I'm afraid."

"Yes, and one Y chromosome too many as well, I suppose."

"Sorry dear. I didn't write the original lyric. You'll have to blame Paul."

And with that the four wiseacres made hastily for the studio.

******

Manus again remained behind, moved an empty chair into position, rested his feet on it, sat back and closed his eyes against the last of the sun.

"You're still not going to join them Caleb? It seems like a cause you could get behind."

"They're not going to save the world with a silly song."

"You never know. You never know what's going to go viral these days. All sorts of odd things suddenly become all the rage. The times are desperate. No use being overly discriminating now. It's, 'throw everything at the wall time and hope something sticks,' Caleb. Whatever it turns about to be, something has to. It simply has to."

"Well I'm sure it has all the characteristics and consistency of a substance likely to stick to a wall. A madhouse wall or a chimpanzee cage."

"It's only a bit of fun Caleb. A bit of play. Why don't you join them?"

"No. I don't play. I've never gone in much for play."

"Why ever not?"

"It's not in my nature I guess."

"Even as a child?"

"Well, it's in the nature of children to play. So I suppose I did, some. I don't remember."

"It's in the nature of most animals to play, Caleb. Birds and mammals, both young and adults. I think I read somewhere even fish engage in play."

"Yes, cards, I think."

"Hmm?"

"Fish. They play cards. Never mind."

"Oh! Fish! Go Fish! Caleb, you made a joke!"

He smiled in spite of himself.

"See? You can play. Humour is nothing if not play. It's a play on words in fact."

She stood.

"C'mon, let's join the boys. I'll teach you how to play the tambourine. It's easy, and I think there's a tambourine part in Hey Jude. And if there's not we'll make one."

"No, really. I don't … I've never felt comfortable doing that kind of stuff."

"Stuff like playing music? Or simply having fun?"

"Either. Both. Vanity of vanities, I guess. All is vanity."

"Oh dear. All that Ecclesiastes nonsense."

She sat down again.

"'They fuck you up your Mom and Dad …'"

"Excuse me?"

"It's a poem. By … oh dear, I forget. I'm shocking with names now … Great friend of Kingsley Amis … Never mind. It'll come to me. 'They fuck you up your Mom and Dad, they don't mean to, but they do.' It was your parents wasn't it? All that Old Testament nonsense? What ever did they do to you, you poor lamb?"

"Well, they survived a war and a famine to have me, so I can't complain too much I guess. Being besieged by the Nazis for a couple of years would tend to leave a mark on anyone's psyche you'd think. Can you imagine terror like that? I can't. It couldn't help but echo down through the years. Fucking up future generations."

"Yes, of course. I worry about the legacy we're leaving for own kids. What kind of terrors are we bequeathing them?"

She reached across the table and patted his hand consolingly.

"I'm sorry for being so glib, Caleb. My parents survived the Blitz. I suppose, being Dutch in those days, your family were Calvinists as well?"

"Still are I assume. If there's anyone left."

"Oh I see. So that's what this is all about then? Calvinism echoing down through the ages? All that dismal 'nothing new under the sun', 'all things are wearisome' bilge?

Don't you know all those old time religions are nothing but the ignorant, terrified ramblings of protohumans? They're like the simple-minded scribblings of credulous children.

We've outgrown them, Caleb. We've evolved. Nothing in the Old Testament has any relevance to our world. And the same goes for your Diogenes and his miserable band of Cynics and their deluded, pessimistic, Ascetic fellow-mopers too. They were all naive, paranoid, raving, depressive, misanthropic lunatics. They needed girlfriends and medication, most of them. They shouldn't be heeded. They should be pitied."

"I'm not a Calvinist and I'm not Diogenes. I don't live in an empty wine barrel. I'm not homeless by choice. If the city hadn't towed my van I would have a home today. I am homeless because I am poor."

"I said you could …" she began.

"I know. Let me finish. The idea that a life led simply and sparingly, that a life devoted to sacrifice for some important personal belief, is somehow lunatic is deeply offensive. Sacrifice is a respected tradition across all faiths, and perfectly common in the secular world too.

You misunderstand me if you think I abstain from the frivolous pursuit of pleasure out of some self-denying religious delusion. I abstain from the so-called 'pleasures' of the world because I believe our civilization is insane. I believe it is morally depraved to continue to live as we do when we know, and have known for decades, that our lifestyles, our pleasures, our modern conveniences, and the very foundations of our societies are suicidal. Homicidal in fact. We all know this. If not consciously, at least subconsciously. This is textbook cognitive dissonance. This is delusion. This is madness. You think the Ascetics were all psych ward cases? Well physician diagnose thyself."

"I'm so sorry, Caleb. It was horrid of me to say those things to you. I was only trying to help, honestly. I guess I just don't see the point in needless suffering when there is still so much beauty and joy to be savoured in this world. As messed up as it is.

We only get one go-round though, why waste it? Every life is a miracle, don't you think? That life of any complex kind exists on this planet at all is mind-boggling to me. I just think we should devote ourselves to celebrating that as much and as often as we can. Which is to say, constantly. Every blooming minute of our existence. That was all I meant to say."

"I know. I wasn't accusing you. You're a very thoughtful, considerate person. That's obvious. We just adhere to different schools of thought, that's all."

He smiled mollifyingly.

"There's no need for you to be sorry. We're simply having a frank exchange of views. I spend as much of my life as I can debating. It's what brings me satisfaction, and I suppose what you would call joy. I live for this. I see a world that is sleepwalking to extinction. I feel it is my obligation, my duty as a human being, to try to rouse as many somnambulists as I can during the life that was gifted me. Even if that number is only one, I feel I will have served my purpose. Can you understand that?"

59

She nodded. Emotion quavered her lips, filled her eyes with tears, and tore at her throat. She only just stopped herself from absurdly forming the sign of the cross. She shook her head almost imperceptibly, blushing, and uttered a syllable of laughter at herself.

Too much wine? Or was it the second hand smoke in the studio? Either way, she must have a good buzz on. Obviously.

"Have you ever heard of a Vietnamese Buddhist monk named Quang Duc?" he asked.

"I don't think so. Why?"

"On June 11th, 1963 Quang Duc assumed the lotus position on a street corner in Saigon, had a fellow monk dump a five gallon can of gasoline over him, and set himself alight."

"Oh my god. Why?"

"Because the Buddhist majority population in South Vietnam was being persecuted by the Catholic Church-supporting government, and the Catholic minority there."

"So what happened?"

"The newspaper photos of the event spread horror around the world. The Kennedy administration withdrew its support for the government, it fell, leading eventually to the war."

"The Vietnam War."

"Right."

"But that's terrible. I don't understand. Millions of people died because of that monk torching himself? Why are you telling me this?"

"One corrupt government fell because of that monk. And the wealthiest, most powerful empire the world has ever known was mortally wounded too by that one lone courageous self-sacrificing monk."

"The last time I looked America was still going."

"Rome wasn't destroyed in a day."

"I still don't get your point."

"Seemingly small acts of self-sacrifice by otherwise anonymous people can have profound, earth-shattering consequences. Do you think that Quang Duc lived a meaningful life?"

"I don't know. I don't know anything about his life but his death. And I honestly don't see much merit in that, I have to say."

Little Diogenes suddenly trotted through the doors onto the patio.

"Oh, poor little Diogenes," she cooed. "The band still won't let you into the studio? Come on. Let's go down to the lawn. You must be desperate for a piddle, and I've got a whole trunk full of doggy play-toys you'll like."

She rose and led Diogenes, his curly little tail wagging happily, to the end of the deck and down the stairs to the backyard.

It was dark when Cass returned to the veranda. She'd received a text from the delivery driver. He was at the gate with their Chinese food. Manus appeared to be fast asleep in his seat at the table. She didn't wake him.

She walked through the house turning on lights, opened the gate and waited at the front door, skillfully holding Little Diogenes inside with the deft, well-practised use of her instep. When she returned to the patio with the food Big Diogenes was nowhere to be seen. She carried the bags into the kitchen and set them on the island. While retrieving plates from the cupboard she glanced down the hall toward the bathroom where she assumed The Pisser was occupied. The door was open and the room was dark.

She sent Alex a text informing him dinner was ready. His phone buzzed at her from the counter next to the wine cooler. She sighed and went downstairs. When she returned she looked again on the deck for Apeman. She stood at the railing and cast her eyes round the darkened lawn as well. Still no sign of him. Huh.

She went back into the kitchen and stood at the island, feeling vaguely alarmed but not quite knowing why. He hadn't been gone for more than a few minutes. It was a big house, the yard was dark. Perhaps he went for a stroll in the garden. Maybe he'd wandered upstairs for some reason …

A shiver of possessiveness immediately ran down her spine. What had she left lying around that was dear and easily pocketed? There were expensive knickknacks everywhere, too numerous to list. Any number of valuable pieces could go missing and their absence might go unnoticed for ages, until it was too late. There was almost certainly money lying around too. And jewelry. Oh god, the jewelry. There was so much of it. And little of it in the safe. She felt sick. And frightened. And guilty.

Warily she climbed the stairs to the upper level. It was entirely dark and still. She crept into the master bedroom and flicked on the light. Nothing. She passed into the walk-in closet and her dressing room. Everything seemed to be in order. All her bling was present and accounted for. Nothing whatever had been disturbed.

Nothing save for her conscience.

When she returned downstairs it was silent and still. No sign of Little Diogenes now either. No click-click-click sound of his untrimmed nails on the tiles. Surely she thought, he can't have vanished too?

"Diogenes?" she called. "Di-og-en-ese." Nothing. "Caleb?"

She went out on the veranda and called into the darkness, "Caleb?" She waited. No response.

Well, this was a mystery. She started to send Alex a text, remembered his phone was sitting next to the wine fridge, and put her phone back in her pocket. Suddenly, unaccountably alarmed, she hurried downstairs to the studio and burst in without knocking. The sheer magnitude of her relief at seeing Alex sitting at the drums with his headphones on, happily playing, almost made her cry. He looked up and grinned at her.

"Is it getting cold?" he shouted. "We'll be right there. I think I've almost got this down."

She smiled wanly and sat on the arm of a chair, feeling faint.

"What's the matter?" he asked, removing his headphones. "Did they get the order wrong again?"

"No. Nothing. It's silly. I think I'm a little drunk. Only I can't find Caleb, and now Little Diogenes seems to have disappeared too."

"Disappeared? What do you mean?"

"I mean gone. Suddenly absent. Missing. Not where they ought to be for no discernible reason."

"Okay, okay. Take it easy honey. We'll find them, they can't have gone far."

"He's probably scarpered," said John. "He does that. One minute he's there, the next, he and Diogenes have buggered off. No warning. No explanation."

"Yeah," agreed Dude. "Ape's not big on goodbyes. He's probably walking back to the park."

"He might have to get his things from the shelter before a certain time," suggested Rog.

"There we are," said Alex. "Several discernible reasons. Let's eat. I'm starving."

******

It was an idyllically warm night and they ate at the table on the deck. Alex and the boys chatted animatedly about the progress of Hey Dude, and they asked him questions about recording techniques and his various songs and any other assorted rock star experiences he cared to share - of which, there were rather a lot.

Cass picked at her food silently, ruminating on some of the things Caleb had said, watching the backyard for a sight of Big Diogenes and/or Little Diogenes emerging from the shadows coming back from the beach.

Suddenly she interrupted Alex in the middle of his story about the time Tom Petty dropped by Jeff Lynne's place for a visit while Lynne was producing Alex's solo record …

"Honey, I've been thinking about the wisdom of promoting a Dudeist-type faith with the world in the state it's in," she said. "I love the Dude, you know I do. I've watched the film nearly as often as you have. But a figure who's belief system never rises much above 'take it easy' isn't really what we need to save ourselves from climate disaster is he? The Dude's philosophy was apropos for the 60's, but surely 'going with the flow' and placidly 'abiding' is not the sort of inspiration we need as we teeter on the brink of extinction.

The time for laid back lamas is passed. We need an active, assertive, philosophically rigorous faith leader. Something like a pope of the proletariat. A figure who'll have empathy and love for the downtrodden and the marginalized. Someone who will lead the fight against the nihilists of the corrupt capitalist order and the petty parochialism of nation states and their myopic focus on sustaining endless economic growth within certain arbitrary borders drawn on a map. We need someone who will lead us beyond the joyless, rapacious, egocentric civilization we've created. Someone who will help to end the estrangement of people from nature, and from the responsibility each of us owes to our fellow human beings. We need someone like …"

"Someone like the Big Diogenes for instance?"

"I was thinking Greta Thunberg, or someone like her. Jacinda Ardern, or Alexandria Ocasio-Cortez, or Naomi Klein maybe. But Caleb is right Alec. You know he is. We all know he is. We're already into runaway climate change. Large parts of the world are already rapidly becoming uninhabitable. Every day it's environmental disaster after environmental disaster, one after another. Fires and droughts, and unimaginable deluges, and flash flooding, and glaciers collapsing, and polar ice sheets melting. Soon, very soon, it will be large scale crop failures and mass starvation and millions upon millions of desperate refugees. Taking it easy is not going to cut it."

Suddenly she heard something.

"Quiet!" she shushed.

They immediately fell silent in alarm and confusion.

"What? What is it?" Alex whispered, rattled. Head-lamped, bicycle riding Fentanyl fiends? he wondered, peering into the darkness.

"I thought I heard something."

They waited, listening.

"There. Did you hear that?"

They trained their ears and waited, not yet caught on to what they were supposed to be listening for.

"I thought I heard a …. There! I did. Little Diogenes! He's barking. Down on the beach!"

"Oh Jesus," Alex exclaimed. "You fucking scared me. I thought … I don't know what I thought. But you freaked me out."

Calmer now he said, "Well, there you are then. You can relax. They went for a walk. Everything is perfectly explicable after all."

"I hear him too," said Rog. "That's definitely Diogenes. I'd know that bark anywhere."

From the northwest came the sound of a train whistle.

"Another coal train?" said John.

"It would be an empty one," said Rog.

"It'll be the Amtrak heading south," said Alex.

They heard it sound again, getting just perceptively louder as it neared. Presently the vibrations from a subsequent, nearer blast caused a slightly greater sensation in their inner ears. And then there came another. And another. And another directly after the last one. And finally one long steady urgent deafening wail of warning.

"Oh my god! Today is June 11th!" Cass exclaimed, springing to her feet.

"Yes it is. What of it?" Alex asked.

"It means he's going to do a Quang Duc!" she cried, running for the stairs.

"Duck?" said Rog, closely inspecting the piece of fowl impaled on his fork. "I thought this was lemon chicken."

Alex, Dude, and John looked at each other, bewildered, forks hovering before their open mouths.

"What the fuck is a kwang duck?" said John.

Alex turned in his chair in time to see Cass disappear across the lawn into the darkness, racing for the stairs to the beach.

"I don't know," he said, standing hastily in alarm, "but we'd better go find out."

They hurried after her.

By the time they reached the top of the stairs the train whistle was a constant insistent scream of distress. Locked-up steel wheels shrieked the sound of the enormous force of emergency-activated friction battling against inertia.

They felt their way down the pitch-black steps as quickly as they dared, gripping the railing for guidance, shouting after her, "Cass!"

The lights of the engine now lit up the tracks and the beach below. They caught a glimpse of Cass nearing the bottom of the stairs, just as the engine and six passenger cars of the evening Seattle-bound Amtrak, whistle bellowing, wheels screeching, sparks flying, thundered past. Several passengers inside the lit car were standing at the windows peering into the night. Others were seated looking braced for potential impact.

Cass was next to the tracks now, hands on her head, close enough to almost reach out and hop aboard. Alex's heart leapt into his throat, all at once gripped by the terror that she was about to jump under its wheels.

"Noooooo!" he screamed.

The train passed, the whistle ceased, and much of the screeching sound of emergency braking abated as it slowed to its eventual stop hundreds of yards down the rails. Shadowy figures jumped to the ground and began to run toward them.

When Alex reached the bottom of the stairs Cass was stumbling around on the tracks peering in desperation into the blackness of the now un-illuminated beach. They reached her all at once, Alex trying to wrap his arms round her as she struggled against him. She was sobbing, wailing.

"We have to find him. Help me find him."

Gingerly they felt their way down the rocky embankment to the shore, and staggered about on the gravel calling out, "Caleb!" "Apeman!" "Diogenes!"

Out of the darkness came the sound of a 'Yip,' and running toward it they then heard a whimper, and suddenly there was Little Diogenes nosing at a dark shape lying prostrate on the ground.

Cass screamed and stopped dead in her tracks. Alex grabbed her and pulled her face against his chest to shield her from the horror. Dude walked slowly over and picked up an unwilling, kicking, Little Diogenes.

John and Rog stood aghast, heads in their hands.

"Oh christ," said John. "Oh christ. What the fuck?"

"Jesus, Caleb," Cass sobbed into Alex's chest. "What have you done? It was only the Amtrak. No one will get it. It'll all be for nothing."

Gently Alex began to slowly lead her away toward the stairs.

"I won't forget Caleb," she sobbed. "Quang Duc, Caleb. I won't forget."

DEATH OF A BOOMER

Norman Wolfe was irritably double-checking his various social media accounts making sure what his assistant had posted for him about his upcoming Open House was accurate. He was a busy man and resented having to take the time to bother over the trifling details of his ads on InstaTwitBook. He paid the girl to look after these things.

But what could he do? He was as reliant on her technological facility as an English-speaking soldier was on a native translator in a foreign war zone, or an Everest climber on a Sherpa. In the modern scope of things he was, at best, semi-literate. A man out of his time. An analog being in a digital age.

The entire concept of 'social media' and any associated terms such as 'devices' or 'platforms' or what-have-you, filled him with loathing. But he knew these were inescapable annoyances of modern business. Something he had to accept and get on with, no matter how much it galled.

So even if she was utterly unreliable and treated him with that maddening "OK Boomer" disdain that more or less explicitly communicated her wish that his generation had died before they got old, he knew it was pointless to replace her. They were all like that these days. The kids aren't alright. And somebody had to do it.

He wearily fired off a text alerting her to the somewhat consequential matter, as Norm saw it, that she'd posted both the wrong address and the wrong time in his ads. Passive aggression thus assuaged, it then it occurred to him, not for the first time, to see if Marion Edwards was a Facebooker.

Apart from advertising his listings and real estate firm, Norm did not use Facebook. He did not post details of his life to his page or his feed or whatever the hell you call it. He did not follow any other person's

67

personal details on it. Nor did he otherwise use it to do business. And he certainly did not rely on it as a source for news or credible information.

As far as he was concerned it was a vehicle for pure evil. A crime against humanity. The delivery system for Vladimir Putin's cyber war and for Donald Trump's presidency; for countless acts of genocide and hatred; for propaganda and disinformation; for personal stalking and harassment and bullying; and for the mind-numbing spread of a global mental health pandemic across all demographics around the world.

But lately, every time he accessed Facebook, the urge to look up Marion would rise in his chest causing a terrifying fight-or-flight response mimicking the symptoms of an arrhythmic tachycardia.

He hadn't seen her or talked to her in forty years. He wasn't sure where she lived, whether she was married and had kids, what she did for a living, or even if she was still alive. He didn't know if she had a Facebook page, or if he'd be able to access it if she did.

But with is heart beating wildly out of control and starting to fear for his disquieted breathing, he decided this time to screw up the courage to try.

No luck. Not under her maiden name anyway.

But after some determined application on the Google machine he discovered her married name and et voila. There she was. Very much alive.

Norm gasped audibly when he saw her profile picture. She looked remarkably like her former 18 year-old self, though an 18 year-old made up as if to play the part of a beautiful matriarch in a school play. Her hair was still long but now highlighted with grey. Her jaw line was softened as though slightly out of focus. Creases like parenthesis framed the corners of her lips. And her eyes, just as he'd remembered, were still so intense and penetrating that, even staring blindly from a screen, he found it daunting to hold her gaze.

It was while his eyes were shyly avoiding hers that his vision alit on her relationship status: 'Single'.

The news stunned him, like an echo of the thunderclap that struck him at his first sight of her 45 years before.

**

It was halfway through the first class of a Monday morning. He was sitting at his desk at the back of Miss Ruffalo's French 8, drawing a series of illustrations at the top right corner of the pages of his Chemistry textbook.

The cartoon character he was drawing was a caped super hero with an enormous nose he called Post Nasal Drip who specialized in mail theft. When the pages of the book were flipped he appeared to fly through the air Superman-style, capturing fleeing mail thieves by pinching a nostril and ensnaring them in vast jets of amber-like snot.

Suddenly, Miss Ruffalo, who had come to that Monday morning's class with refreshed determination to finally get Robert Holland to say correctly, in French, "My name is Robert Holland, and I am thirteen years-old," fell silent.

Norm looked up expecting to find her glaring at him again, but instead saw that the door at the front of the room had opened and Marion was entering hesitantly holding a note from the office in her outstretched hand. His giggling immediately ceased.

Her hair was long and lustrous and dark as midnight, parted simply in the middle, and hanging straight almost to the small of her back. Skin-tight blue jeans hugged slim, adorably knock-kneed legs. And perhaps most startling of all to 13 year-old Norm, in an obvious attempt at concealing precociously developed breasts, she'd draped herself in a too-large replica jersey of his favourite hockey team - the Montreal Canadiens! The storied red home sweater! Les bleu, blanc, et rouge! Le Club de Hockey Canadien!

He gaped at her in astonishment. Behold, what manner of girl is this whom fate has given to us, that she should like hockey!

Oh my god, he heard himself say. Mon Dieu.

Miss Ruffalo read the note and announced "Permettez-moi de vous presenter Marion" and showed her to a desk down front.

"Bonjour Marion," they all chimed, including, uncharacteristically, Norm.

As she turned she cast a brief shy glance up at a sea of faces, but he was sure her eyes met his. Her irises were brown and lively and intelligent. His pupils were dilated. Holy.

All at once his heart couldn't seem to decide whether to race or come to a stop. A sudden terror gripped him like a vague intuition had begun to take shape in his conscious mind for the first time that he was a minuscule being on a large spinning rock hurtling through space at unimaginable speed careening away from the Big Bang.

And further, this sensation of helpless vertigo was symptomatic too of an unenlightened, subconscious notion that his heart, encased in its fragile cage, should be suddenly, rightfully gripped by the fear that the accelerating pace of this platform of space detritus may at any moment spin out of control and career off its orbit, collide with an extinction-event-sized meteor, or get sucked into a vast as yet undiscovered black hole.

None of these astronomical concepts did come to his conscious mind of course. Norm was decidedly no budding Albert Einstein or Carl Sagan. He was merely a bit of a silly kid with a sometimes tenuous grasp of objective reality and a growing penchant for romanticism and an ever-expanding inventory of morbid fears.

Back in the real world, Norm fixed his eyes on his desk top and willed himself to calm down. Focus. He wasn't daydreaming. This was really happening. The most perfect girl in the world had just walked into his grade 8 French class. Here, in this armpit of a fishing village in the middle of nowhere.

A Canadian nowhere.

And as he well knew, as far as nowheres went, this was out there.

Suddenly the existence or nonexistence of god almost seemed an actual thing. A vision appeared to his mind's eye of a giant Terry Gilliam-animated hand of god from a Monty Python skit, and Michelangelo's Sistine Chapel, reaching down, index finger extended, as though indicating to him: Here she is. The girl you would've prayed for, if you'd prayed. Now what are you gonna do about it?

For to whom do atheists direct their praise for miracles, wondrous coincidences, or cosmic flukes if not a god? Even though they firmly believe one doesn't exist? If there is always a need to assign blame for every calamitous misfortune, then surely someone has to get the credit for each instance of inexplicable good fortune. It seemed to be a part of the architecture of the human mind, the ingrained disposition to credit every instance of blind good luck to some all-powerful, all-seeing divine being, however farcical.

If Norm had been at all susceptible to such religious feeling, he may have acted then with the conviction that it was divine providence that directed this angel into his world. For it would certainly be the will of any God worth believing in that he and Marion's orbits should collide. And thus imbued with the fervour of Heavenly inspired certitude, at the first opportunity, he would've simply, boldly, walked right up to her and begun his courtship, leading inexorably to their shared supernaturally determined fate of going forth and multiplying together, for ever and ever, amen.

Trouble was, Norm was no more receptive to magical thinking than he was to eighth grade French. And so he allowed his unfocused gaze to pan slowly out the window and to settle on the progress across the sky of some large puffy clouds (of the Cumulous Mediocris species, not that Norm was at all knowledgable on cloud types) while he silently, but without much conviction, began to rehearse what he might say as soon as the class was over and he could get near her.

Nothing good came immediately to mind.

"So, you're a Canadiens fan too, eh?" made him blush in embarrassment just thinking it.

"Who's your favourite player?" seemed somehow even more lame.

And in any case, he didn't want to talk to her about Guy Lafleur or Ken Dryden or Larry Robinson. He wasn't entirely sure what he wanted to talk to her about. But it definitely wasn't that.

But, faint heart never won fair lady and all that, so for the first time in his life he set his mind on a determined course and persisted.

In aid of this he fixed his eyes on the back of her head as though hoping that by concentrating hard enough he might work some kind of Vulcan mind meld and thereby gain some clue from hacking into her innermost thoughts as to what combination of words would work on her.

But staring hard for some minutes brought him no melding of minds and no useful lines. Just a prematurely world-weary feeling that he'd rolled up to the gates of her skull in a Trojan horse and she'd failed to even notice and let him in.

Before long the idea that staring at the back of her head might bring about some inspiring pick-up lines seemed absurd even to him.

Besides, when Spock worked a Vulcan mind meld he didn't stare creepily at the back of someone's head. He gripped his subject by the face with both hands like a basketball player preparing to put up a free throw. The idea was stupid. It couldn't work. And Norm hated Star Trek anyway.

71

So once again, he resignedly let his gaze drift out the adjacent window and idly noticed that the clouds seemed to be scudding across the sky much more quickly that day.

Little did Norm know that by concentrating so hard on coming up with the perfect pick-up line, the closer he'd come in a way, to adding a new wrinkle to Newton's Third Law of Motion, which posited that for every action there is an equal and opposite reaction. Norm's amendment, had he ever heard of Isaac Newton, would've been that the more force one applies in thought, the mind blanks in equal and opposite measure.

He glanced at the clock above the chalkboard. The bell would soon go. He had to come up with something that wasn't completely fucking stupid to say to her in the hallway on the way to Social Studies. If he could get near her.

Finally, just as he was settling in desperation on the only two irony-dripping possibilities his addled mind could come up with - either, "Come here often?" Or, "Are you married? Would you like to be?" he was punched painfully in the bicep.

"Ow. Shit. Two minutes for roughing."

His best friend Jeremy grinned at him.

"Whoa, eh?! Thank. You. God."

Ow shit indeed.

At thirteen most kids are aware the ultimate measure of privilege in life is to be good-looking. Forget cleanliness, it's attractiveness that's next to godliness. To be judged more physically appealing by your peers in high school is to feel the sun shines out of your nether regions.

Norm was acutely aware of this fact. So was Jeremy.

Jeremy was blond, blue-eyed, athletic, extroverted, and humorous. He was generally assumed by Norm and his male classmates to be the popular object of the adolescent fantasies of all the girls of their year. Doubtless many of the girls in the higher grades too. And possibly a few of the teachers.

Students of both sexes parted in the hallways to let him pass. Teachers favoured him. Referees favoured him. He would've been most favoured of god if he'd existed.

He was the budding local equivalent of the Robert Redford-type. Picture Jeremy as The Sundance Kid to Norm's Butch Cassidy - if Butch had been played by Richard Dreyfus rather than Paul Newman.

So Jeremy's interest in Marion was not only inevitable as Norm now saw, but also fatal to his congenitally faint heart.

For even if Jeremy hadn't been a preternaturally confident sure-fire future Adonis statue in the making, he was also the son of the local Anglican Minister and therefore no doubt open to actually believing that a supreme deity would reach down from the clouds or Mount Olympus or some such divine place and purposely put this beautiful girl into his path.

When Jeremy thanked god you suspected he really meant it, with a capital G. Because of course he'd believe in a Being occupying some ultimate celestial tier interfering in the mortal world to play favourites. His very existence was proof of this.

In Jeremy's world the meek didn't inherit the earth, the meek got what was left over after the blessed few grasped all they could get their arms around. Like human civilization itself really, from religion, to monarchies, to aristocracies, to income tax laws. History was a long cruel succession of trickle-down theory made manifest, long before Ronald Reagan's Voodoo Economics of four years hence.

Norm knew instinctively that, though he'd only known Marion even existed for a few brief transcendent moments, he would have no chance with her. She belonged amongst the lofty. She was objectively out of his league. If Jeremy wanted her he'd get her. And he wanted her. Of course he wanted her.

So, when the bell tolled finis on the class it was Jeremy who strolled Moses-like through parting, queuing classmates and introduced himself to her. They walked out the door together chatting amiably while Norm loitered at the back of the room pretending an urgent need to rearrange the textbooks in his Adidas bag and pondering what would have amounted to, in a more clinical, scientific mind, pioneering thinking on the as yet unwritten theory of depressive realism.

***

Norm loved this view. When he'd bought up all this denuded former timberland twenty years before people had thought he was crazy.

Who'd want to live way up there so far from town, up on a barren hillside that looked like it was afflicted with mange, with a bird's eye view of a sulphurous, smoke-spewing pulp mill? It was a wasteland overlooking a dark satanic mill. Gross.

Well, the mill was long gone and in its place was a pleasant little seaside strata development Norm had marketed himself. The profits he realized from this project he then funnelled into his most ambitious development, Olympian Heights, which took the place of the hillside wasteland.

And now Norm could sit on his flagstone patio next to his pool, a Colossus at rest, and look down over the city and the harbour and all the little people and cars and boats moving about down there.

And from here too he was afforded an elevated perspective overlooking the surrounding homes of The Heights as well. From here he could look down on everybody. And nobody could look down on him.

For he saved the highest, largest, most exclusive lot in the subdivision for himself. Then he hired the hottest architectural firm on the west coast to design him a palace. And boy howdy, did they. Ten thousand square feet of marble, and glass, and stone, and recycled hundred year-old handcrafted beams, and palm trees, and waterfalls, and an almost Olympic-sized pool, and well, Zeus himself would live here if he could.

They had also said he was crazy for building a house like this. Not 'they' as in the architects and contractors of course, but 'they' as in his friends and colleagues at his firm.

You can't build a place like that in this town, they all warned him. It's like a friggin' temple. It's a blue collar burg, they won't take to somebody lording over them like that. They'll take it out on the business. They won't list with you. They won't buy from you. They'll shun you out of town for spite and spit on you as you flee in disgrace.

But they were wrong.

He smiled to himself looking down from these majestic heights, as he always did when he recalled how he got to here from whence he came.

People won't like you lording over them? Yeah right. People wanted desperately to be lorded over. They worshipped useless, parasitic inbred royals; and pop stars who couldn't sing in tune or play an instrument; and narcissistic athletes; and megalomaniacal tech titans; and fascistic politicians; and television evangelists; and raging, hyperventilating YouTube dimwits; and celebrity chefs; and inane, talentless social media 'influencers;' and on and on and on and on. People were so desperate to be lorded over they allowed the single most despicable human being on the planet to become its most powerful person for four long, long years.

So Norm ignored his friends and colleagues and went all-in on conspicuous consumption.

He wore suits that cost more than most people's cars. He drove cars that cost as much as most people's houses. When he hired the scornful girl to set up and manage his social media accounts, most people he knew had barely heard of the term 'social media'. When he employed a videographer to film videos of his listings for his own YouTube channel, most other realtors thought of YouTube as a mere repository for cat videos and stupid human fails.

But he made sure the camera's lens was focused on himself and his custom made Italian suits in every video. And he made sure his Maserati featured prominently parked in the driveway of every ad too.

People wouldn't like it? His videos developed a large following of subscribers and generated thousands of clicks and shares. People were impressed by it. People respected it. People ate this shit up. Norm's sales soared exponentially.

Others saw a clearly gifted and imaginative anticipator of coming trends. Someone who had demonstrated a deft grasp of the vision thing. And people will follow those rare beings who possess vision. Into a subdivision or over a cliff, it makes no difference. Get out in front of them, show them a way - any way - and they'll tag along, grateful for not having to think for themselves.

Norm knew it was all bullshit of course. The Maserati. The dyed blond hair. The tight suits. The stupid pontoon-shaped Italian loafers that pinched his feet and gave him painful ingrowing toenails. But when he walked into a room he turned heads. Women wanted to fuck him. Men wanted to give him their money.

It was all a transparent confidence trick of course. A scam. But capitalism itself is a scam, an enormous Ponzi scheme. The entire basis of human civilization was a fraud built upon the systematic Pavlovian training of the credulous masses to esteem charlatans and crap and to fall for endless pump-and-dump schemes.

From Bronze Age gods, to medieval kings, to Wall Street titans, to Silicone Valley techno-fascists, it was all the same con. If enough people could be persuaded some dubious thing was true, then, for all intents and purposes, it was. Or may as well be. And if two-fifths of the population were dumb enough not to heed the warnings of climate scientists or epidemiologists, then it was a small matter to get rich by convincing enough gullible people to invest in stock markets weighted overwhelmingly in favour of insiders and institutional investors. Or to invest real capital in virtual currencies. Or in Norm's case, to buy houses they couldn't possibly afford in an over extended bubble market.

Lure 'em in with visions of exclusive affluence. Take their money. Inflate the bubble. Reap the profits at the point of maximum expansion. Burst the bubble. Descend like vultures on the ruins. Rinse and repeat. The long sought meaning of life, the universe, and everything wasn't 42 as Douglas Adams had it, but simple, brutal, cannibalism. The amoral triumph of the select few at the top of the food chain to prey upon the desperate, the naive, the envious, and the weak.

And at this point, nearing the end of humanity's timeline, what else was there? What possible difference could it make to a world gone mad if Norm exploited these mass delusions too? This was his stall at Homo sapiens' great going-out-of-business bazaar and he was simply working it. Making a buck. Earning his bread. Taking his seat at the all-you-can-consume civilizational feeding frenzy. Call it what you will. But there's a reason they call it making a living. If you're not busy getting rich you may as well get busy getting dead.

So he didn't feel too guilty about what some others would call the 'excesses' of his lifestyle and carbon footprint. The vast majority of people were as destructive and single-mindedly rapacious as a plague of locusts. Everyone wanted what he had and would destroy heaven and earth to get it. Hell, they were destroying heaven and earth to get it.

Norm was no climate change denier. He could see it was plainly evident and was already causing serious environmental effects. But what's more, he could see that it was too late to avert catastrophe. There was simply no appetite to do much of anything about it, even if something could be done about it. There was no chance to abruptly alter human nature.

Once upon a time the world's dominant economic model had been based on human slavery. That exploitation had been superseded by one dependant on fossil fuels. It had taken hundreds of years of righteous opposition before the weight of the moral depravity of human slavery caused its downfall. Humanity didn't have hundreds of years to work with in overthrowing the immoral fossil fuel-powered capitalist economic system.

The climate criminals and the growing authoritarian, undemocratic political movements they funded and perpetuated had most of the money, nearly all the guns, and no real compelling need to alter their genocidal business model. There was still a lot of money to be made. And so much money already invested in existing infrastructure. We're talking trillions of dollars. No one is going to walk away from those kind of profits or write off those sorts of losses. Not without a fight. And who was going to make them? Extinction Rebellion? Greenpeace? The United Nations? Greta Thunberg? George Monbiot? Yeah right. Pull the other one.

So, you know. Fuck it. If civilization is doomed anyway what's the harm in stoking and profiting from a real estate bubble? Or a stock market bubble? Or a cryptocurrency bubble? Or another bloody Dutch tulip bulb market bubble for that matter.

You want to talk about bubbles? Human civilization was the ultimate bubble. Seven and a half billion greedy souls - wait, what time is it? Maybe it's eight billion by now - competing for survival on a planet capable of sustainably supporting a quarter as many. That was the bubble to end all bubbles right there.

So you may as well enjoy yourself before it goes bang right? Norm was in his late 50's now. His time was almost up. If all the various economic blisters could keep inflated for 15 or 20 more years, for his intents and purposes, it would be like the inevitable burst never happened. Because it wouldn't have. Not to him anyway. The noxious puss of the cataclysmic popping will splatter all over somebody else. All the poor buggers who have the misfortune to survive him. And, well, not to be too cynical or anything, but that will be their problem. What could he do about it? He didn't dream this nightmare into reality. He simply lived by its tenets - and profited from them.

And anyway, what did he know? He may have shown a talent for a certain narrow, intuitive financial sagacity, but he wasn't all-seeing. He wasn't infallible. Maybe a solution was possible. Maybe there was a chance at a miracle awaiting. Some technological or philosophical salvation coming in the last act to save humanity.

It could happen. He tried to believe that whenever he felt the need of it. You had to didn't you? To get out of bed in the morning. To keep going.

But either way he knew it didn't really concern him. For Norm had also demonstrated the foresight not to have procreated. Having no kids was not only environmentally friendly, it was also a boon for the conscience. He could live large with no qualms.

One day his perspective would simply go black. Snuffed out like Tony Soprano's POV by the man in the Member's Only Jacket. Except he would leave behind no Carmela. No Meadow. Not even an Anthony Junior. It was a comforting thought. Especially not leaving behind an Anthony Junior. How did Tony not smother him with a pillow like he tried to smother his mother Livia? Why did he save him from the pool? Whiny little shit.

He got up and went inside, poured himself a refill, and returned to his chair. Far below in the darkness the strobe-like red and blue lights of a couple of police cars signalled their path through the city, wending their way silently through the streets of the downtown core. It was like a light show performed every night just for him and the lesser gods of The Heights.

Everywhere these days it seemed the streets were infested with more and more homeless people. Filthy, shambling, impudent, ungrateful welfare cases. Passed out on the steps of the bank. Choking up the sidewalks with their flea-bitten mutts and their shopping carts piled high with mouldering bed-bugged belongings. Desecrating the War Memorial Park with their tents and cardboard lean-tos and their pissing and shitting. Draining the resources of the emergency services with their property crimes, their overdoses, their beatings, their murders, and their suicides. Driving up the taxes of all the law-abiding wealth-creators.

It was abominable what took place down there. Shameful really. And regrettable too, he would acknowledge that. Norm often wondered why they didn't simply load up a syringe and end it all. Why suffer needlessly like that? What was the point when it would be so easy to return to the nothingness from which you sprung before your birth? It would be the rational thing to do. The most merciful consummation to be wished. There simply wasn't enough wealth to go around. There were just too many extraneous people. And you can only really afford to live as long as you can, well, afford to live. That was axiomatic.

What could he or anyone else do about it? Watch it all play out and feel bad?

Well, he would watch, but he'd be damned if he'd feel bad.

From Norm's elevated vantage point the unravelling of society made for compulsive viewing. And if it's there playing out in front of you, for free no less, why not watch? If you didn't think about it too much it could be entertaining. An innocent distraction from fears of real estate crashes, debt crises, global pandemics, cyberwarfare, nuclear holocaust, global warming - death.

Besides, there was nothing that made him feel more powerful and successful than, at the end of another productive, lucrative day, sitting above it all sipping a vintage single malt and watching the light show and feeling satisfied and grateful for his blessings.

Down there the cretins crept like time in their petty pace from day to day on their way to dusty death. They were the shadows, the poor players, and those dismal streets were the stage they strutted upon. It was a tale of idiots, told by idiots, broadcast to idiots. Just like reality TV and YouTube and social media. Full of fury, but from this high remove, robbed of its sound. Up amongst these gated streets he could sit and watch and hear nothing but the pool gurgling and the sound of his own thoughts.

Yes, he reflected, Sartre was right, c'est exact, hell *is* other people. Consider the pandemic. Idiots gormlessly parading around without masks on. Refusing to get vaccinated. Protesting easy and simple health regulations that would've saved untold amounts of wealth, not to mention lives.

Masses of morons loudly professing their faith in 'Q' and wearing MAGA hats - in Canada! This was batshit mental behaviour in America for christ's sake. For citizens of other countries to be emulating this kind of lunacy made you long for extinction. Time was, people would go to great lengths to conceal their imbecility. Now they broadcast it to the world on Facebook and Instagram, and on tee shirts and baseball caps and truck bumpers.

He could feel his pulse beginning to throb and his blood pressure rising. He knew he shouldn't let himself get so worked up about all this shit. Once or twice lately the rhythm of his heart had suddenly felt like an engine with a broken motor mount threatening to rev out of control. Like something inside could snap or blow or flip. He told himself to just concentrate on the sound of the pool filters at work. Gurgle, gurgle, gurgle. Ommm.

Think happy thoughts.

The pandemic had been very good for him. Very, very good. He'd be the first to admit he hadn't seen that one coming. When the world was first driven into lockdown he was sure the markets would crash - both real estate and money markets. He'd thought at the time the end was nigh. That this was the inevitable collapse and that he'd waited too long to cash out.

And yet, here they were one short year later and he'd never had so good a year as this last one. The world was going mad, the pandemic was raging, violence the world over seemed to be spiralling out of control.

Suddenly everyone wanted to live in Canada. People were desperate to buy here. Or to invest here, to park their money here, at any rate. There were huge profits to be had. Detached house prices soared. Sales were record-breaking, through the roof. Deals often done remotely. Unconditional offers made site-unseen, thousands over the asking. His biggest problem suddenly was finding enough properties to satisfy the demands of buyers - and he and most of his colleagues were run off their feet processing new listings.

Still, as problems go, these were nice ones to have. He was grateful. Exhausted. But grateful.

Still his heart wouldn't settle down. Find your happy place.

He picked up his phone and checked in on Marion's Facebook page. He'd been doing this all day. Seeing pictures of her never failed to give his heart what it seemed to need. First, a jolting jump-start of sudden unalloyed joy followed by a warm soothing sensation as though her image or his memories of her were liquified and loaded up in a needle and cranked into his veins. Pure bliss.

Ah, Emmy. That was what he'd called her. M.E: Marion Edwards. At last he'd found something that made him feel comfortably numb.

It was then he noticed from her feed a reference to the fact that their class's 40th reunion was on for Canada Day weekend.

Ordinarily, the only thing Norm loathed more than other people's weddings was the idea of high school reunions. He'd been to a couple of his ex-wife's, and to a few more with various girlfriends. They'd all been thoroughly dismal occasions. No one ever seemed to actually enjoy them.

He'd never been to one of his own of course. Directly out of school he'd traded one coast for the opposite one, putting as many miles between the past and the present as it was geographically possible. And since then he'd never been back, hadn't kept in touch with any of his old friends, and couldn't remember the last time he'd given them or his old hometown a thought. At least before he discovered Emmy's Facebook page. And now it seemed he could think of little else.

And so, it seemed, Norm had heard the siren call of the high school reunion. He was going home.

****

The most awe-inspiring image Norm had ever seen was the famous 'Earth Rise' photo taken from Apollo 8. From the perspective of the moon's orbit the Earth was a truly wondrous creation. Unutterably sublime. The most perfect heaven that has ever existed in this or any other known galaxy.

In 1968 National Geographic had reproduced the photo in poster-size and included it in the following edition, and Norm had tacked it to his bedroom wall and marvelled at it endlessly for years afterward.

Of course, being but a lad and not a particularly curious or intellectually inclined one at that, he couldn't know what certain Bronze Age philosophers may have thought heaven consisted of. But if he had, then surely this was more like it.

No other garden was necessary. Here was proof. QED. It wasn't god or Jesus or Mohammed or Joseph Smith or L Ron Hubbard who ascended to heaven, it was us. We were already there. Every blessed creature on Earth had attained paradise simply by being born. How had we not shucked off the surly bonds of ignorant, pre-enlightenment superstition and realized what was so bleeding obvious? What was the fault in us that prevented this idea from catching on?

Fifty years later Norm wasn't often reminded of the Earth Rising image. The poster gave up its wall space eventually to White Album and Abbey Road keepsakes, and Farrah Fawcett pictures, and Montreal Canadiens photos, and Vancouver Canuck calendars, and Liverpool Football Club banners.

It hadn't sparked a philosophic or spiritual revolution of any great import. It retained something of its symbolic cache amongst environmentalists. But in the general public's imagination it became a visual cliche, one of scores of images of the little blue marble in its infinite wine-dark sea. What powers of inspiration it may once have held now more often fired the arguments of Flat-Earthers who claimed the picture was a hoax staged on a Hollywood film set.

But for all Norm's childhood idealism and nascent Gaia-ism the most awe-inspiring view he could imagine now was the one laid out before him outside his cabin window. A world wrapped for safe keeping in cotton batting. He never tired of it, and never missed a chance to fly. He seemed to spend half his life acquiring frequent flyer points and the other half using them up.

He signalled for another drink and looked out the window with the satisfaction of knowing that his life consisted of nothing but metaphorically, and often literally, soaring above the clouds in a Boeing-built winged chariot, basking in the endless sunshine of First Class. There was absolutely nothing to be worried about. All was well now, at the present time; all will be well in a future present time. That's the way it has been, therefore that is the way it will always be. For ever and ever, amen.

The stewardess stopped to serve a young couple seated in front of him, and as the man reached for his drink his earbud fell out and Norm heard the soft but unmistakable sound of a strumming guitar and Dylan's voice nasalling:

'As the present now/ Will later be past/ The order is rapidly fading/ And the first now/ Will later be last/ For the times they are a-changin'.'

He smiled. Such a quaint notion. Funny how it continues to persist.

✳✳✳✳

It had taken a while, but Norm had finally gotten to know her. She'd hung out with Jeremy for the first couple of months after that first day, causing he and Jeremy to effectively cease being best friends. They still played hockey together and joked around a bit in class, but it was awkward.

Emmy was friendly toward Norm. She was friendly toward everyone. She was in every sense a lovely girl. But he couldn't overcome his shyness around her. His mind went blank whenever she talked to him. And seeing how easy and comfortable a friendship she and Jeremy had immediately fallen into, felt to Norm like someone with a dull scalpel

82

had opened his chest and poured salt on his heart. And so he did his best to discreetly avoid them as much as he could.

Then one day Jeremy was absent, sick. And while he was away Emmy began to hang out exclusively with Norm.

Amazingly, she just sat down next to him that day in the library and started talking to him. Afterward she accompanied him back to class. Then sat next to him in the next class, and the one after that, and the one after that. From that day on they began walking into town every lunchtime for fries and gravy and sugary coffee at The Ship's Inn. And, oh my god, she began to call him on the phone in the evenings and chatter away happily while he mostly grinned and listened, puce with embarrassment, his sweaty hand clutching the receiver of the immobile rotary phone, as his parents sat mere feet away pretending to watch 60 Minutes or All in the Family, listening intently to what few words he muttered in return.

When Jeremy returned to school after a week or ten days or so, he returned to a different universe. Emmy and Norm's new friendship carried on as before and it was now Jeremy who avoided them. In fact, he suddenly seemed to avoid everyone. He even abruptly moved away from them down to the front of all their classes. And he stopped going into town at lunch and rather stayed behind in the gym shooting free throws by himself.

Norm was sorry his friend was so jealous. He knew after all what it felt like when their roles were reversed, and was relieved now not to have to endure the slug-death heart pains that made him dread school and despair of life itself.

But he could admit it now 45 years later, he felt not a little triumphant that god's gift to girls, the golden idol Jeremy, was so suddenly transformed into a sullen, ashen-faced drag.

One day Norm and Emmy were sitting together in the library at one end of a long empty table, facing each other. Having already been shushed several times for laughing, they were now sitting forward in their chairs, craning their chests forward across the table top until they could've rubbed noses. Emmy's brown eyes were wide and alive and dancing with a kind of spirit of joy, or youth, or some ineffable thing that Norm did not yet know how to describe or understand. He knew only that seeing himself reflected in her eyes made him want to live forever.

Just then the library door opened. They both looked toward the sound of intrusion as though startled to learn that time in the rest of the world had not come to a stop.

It was Jeremy. He saw their two laughing faces turn toward him in unison. And he saw too the mirth drain immediately from Emmy's eyes. He spun on his heel and walked right back out.

"Oops," Norm said, grinning.

Emmy immediately shrank back in her chair and fixed him with a look of such profound sadness it made his smile run away for shame.

"What is it? What's going on?

She said nothing, merely stared at him dolefully.

"What's up with him anyway?"

She glanced quickly around the room, leaned across the table, and hushed, "You can't tell anybody about this, okay? No one. Ever."

"Of course. What?"

She stared at the table for a long moment while composing a careful reply.

"There was nothing going on between us. You know. Like that. We were just friends - I just wanted us to be friends. But …"

She looked up at him, steadily. Right in the eyes. And said no more.

He couldn't hold her gaze, he had to look away in confusion. He didn't get it. What did she mean? He asked her out and she said no, she just wanted to be friends. Is that it? But. But what?

The bell sounded before he could ask. They parted wordlessly and went to their respective classes. Afterward she avoided the locker room where he waited for her and went directly to the bus and went home.

Mystified, he wandered down to the beach, sat on a rock and smoked and watched the fishing boats return from the sea. Gradually he began to piece together what seemed a likely explanation for what had transpired and was able to feel that he too, as it were, had returned from being at sea.

Norm decided that when Jeremy had asked her out and she'd said no, telling him she just wanted to be friends, the shock of never before experiencing rejection must've shattered him. Then when he came back to school after being sick and found she'd started hanging out with his best friend he was too embarrassed and angry to speak to either of them.

Clearly, the gist of the whole thing was, Emmy was warning Norm about trying to get too close to her. She was signalling to him that she just wanted to be friends, and that if he tried to ask her out and remake their relationship into something more, she'd do to him what she'd done to Jeremy. Only for Norm it would be worse. If she'd pole-axed Jeremy like that, left their school's Alpha Male a morose, pitiful, whipped dog, what could she do to him? She'd leave him straight-jacketed and babbling in a rubber room, basting in his own filth.

And so he took Jeremy's example and her warning to heart. The next day they resumed their friendship as before. They never mentioned Jeremy or what had happened between them again. During the summer before the start of grade nine Jeremy's family moved away, they never heard or asked where, and he was forgotten. Norm and Emmy remained the best of friends for most of the rest of high school, only drifting apart in their final year when she started to date a slightly older guy who'd finished school and worked at the fish packers.

He never told her he loved her. He never told anyone he loved her. Even though loving her, being with her, making her laugh, had been all that he'd been sure he ever wanted to do. He'd just wanted to be a part of her life somehow. And if a merely platonic relationship had been the price he had had to pay to share a few years of her life it had seemed worth it.

But now he wasn't so sure. It seemed he was still paying the price of not telling her. And the price of not knowing what she would've said had she known was too much. What value did those few years hold now that they were so dimmed by fading memory? He'd have been better off getting dumped by her like Jeremy. He lost her anyway. At least if he'd tried and failed he may have gotten over it and forgotten her. Instead of endless worthless wondering about what might have been.

Norm stared out the window at the clouds obscuring the view of some place or other. Saskatchewan maybe? Even though he was in effect flying into the future, flying from the Pacific time zone to the Atlantic time zone, the time change he felt he was undergoing was 40 years into the past rather than 4 hours into the future.

His life had been greatly impacted by his cravenness. He was by nature, he knew, a diffident, ineffectual, dreamy introvert. A born romantic. A confirmed idealist. He'd once really believed that all you needed was love. He'd known this since that day he'd first laid eyes on Emmy in Miss Ruffalo's French class. And if he could've had his pick of all possible fates, he would've opted for a quiet life spent with her in a sunny little house with a wide view of the sea.

But he hadn't the courage to act on his convictions. He ignored the certainty of his own intelligence and intuition. He'd known forty years before what he still knew today. She was his salvation, his chance at a contented life, and he pusillanimously turned away from it. It was as catastrophic to his own life he thought now, possibly absurdly, as the world turning away from tackling Global Warming after the Rio Earth Summit Conference in 1992.

A better future had once been possible. If only we could go back in time and do things right.

Lifting his gaze from the clouds to the upper reaches of the troposphere and beyond he considered the possibility that somewhere in the infinite reaches of space there may be a planet in a galaxy where humanity had had the wisdom to combat the climate crisis, and Norm had had the guts to tell Emmy he loved her.

But in this one, he knew, of all the CO_2 emissions emitted since 1751, fully half have been released in the past 30 years. And equally as disastrous, in purely selfish terms, he had spent almost the entire span of his time in existence without the woman who would've made that life worth living.

Norm closed his eyes and tried to will that young man's ear bud to fall out again so that he might be freed from a bit of dialogue that would not stop running as though on a loop in his brain. It was a line Diane uttered in an old episode of Cheers, quoting some poet or advertising copywriter or other: "For all sad words of tongue and pen, the saddest are these, 'It might have been.'"

God, shut up.

With an effort Norm willed himself back to the real world and concentrated his mind on the compensatory advantages he'd gained by the loss of Emmy.

By acknowledging and deliberately working to overcome his teenage diffidence he'd made himself over into the sort of glib, back-slapping personality who could become a successful salesman.

Sure, he often felt himself a fool strutting his provincial stage in what he imagined to be the costume of a European sophisticate. As ostentatiously pretentious in his choice of dress as he was in the cars he drove, or the designer knickknacks and modern art with which he filled his astronomically mortgaged mansion.

And yes, the long succession of relationships with women who all bore a superficial physical resemblance to Emmy had lately palled somewhat. But they had been diverting for a long time, as well as being valuable sources of pride and self-confidence. He maintained a place in his memory for them all, a tiny portion of his amygdala perhaps where, like on a shelf in a trophy room displaying plaques for regional sales superiority, he often went to inspect them and to reassure himself of past triumphs.

So to hell with 'what might have been.' The lack of it had made him the man he was today - rich. And by the terms of the modern world there could be no greater accomplishment. It was just one of life's little ironies that he owed the ambition that created that success to his former cowardice.

So rather than wallowing in lamentation for some banal unrequited adolescent love, he should bask in the achievement of a productive life well lived. That was the rational, unsentimental way of thinking anyway. Things have a way of working out for the best. Get over it.

But.

But? Jesus! Always lately with the mood swings.

The closer he got to home the more he began to doubt this sort of rationalizing. The closer he got to home the more certain he became that he knew the meaning of life 40 years before, and that it hadn't changed at all. And nor had he.

He realized now why he might've begun to follow Emmy on Facebook. For even though he hadn't consciously thought about it, he had to have realized on some level that this was the year of their 40th high school reunion. If anyone remembered him and were minded to search for him, they wouldn't know how to find him after all these years. And, what with the pandemic and all, they probably weren't too sure about inviting people from away to return home, and may not bother even searching for him.

So surely there had to be some kind of kismet at work! Not that he believed in kismet. Or was it karma? He was never quite sure what either of those 'K' words actually meant. But regardless, the accidental, coincidental nature of it all thrilled him and seemed to suggest some deeper meaning or purpose to existence - as ridiculous as that thought was.

If he hadn't suddenly begun following Emmy online he would never have known about the reunion, nor would he have learned that she was single too. So sure, there was probably nothing supernatural about it. But it was pretty bloody fortuitous. And he'd take that.

Maybe second acts were possible in Canadian lives. Maybe you could go home again. Hell, maybe there was even a god. Whatever dubious inference there was for Norm to take and pretend to believe from this, one thing was certain. He'd been given the chance to ostensibly go back in time and make right what he had gotten so wrong 40 years before. He was going to seize this opportunity and walk into that Legion Hall, stride right up to Emmy and ask her to marry him right there on the spot.

Well, maybe not right there on the spot. No sense getting carried away. But eventually. Before the weekend was over. Possibly. That much was certain.

The thought brought a little unwitting yip of glee out of him. He flashed an abashed glance round the cabin should anyone have been startled by his outburst, had a long sip of a surprisingly decent single malt, and beamed out the window at this most perfect of all possible worlds.

On arrival in Halifax he grabbed his carry-on from the overhead, bolted through the airport, hurried through the Covid screening, picked up his rented Caddy, and sped for home.

It had been 40 years of wandering in a proverbial desert and he was pleased to see surprisingly little had changed now that he had returned. A few minutes clear of the city and it was mostly two lanes roads, fields, cows, rocky shores, and the vast white-capped expanse of Joyce's snot-green sea stretching out into the infinite, drawing him on as though he were a salmon returning to spawn. Or as Gordon Lightfoot's baritone crooned from the satellite music station, ... 'for the old man has come home, from the forest ...'

The town when he reached it was largely the same, though it had been gentrified. The ages-old buildings of the downtown were brightly painted and adorned by hanging baskets cascading lurid shows of flowers. The streets were lined with expensive cars sporting American license plates, while the sidewalks were thronged with tanned faces, mirrored sunglasses, sun hats, and scarlet arms and legs.

Scores of pleasure craft glinted and bobbed at anchor in the harbour where the fishing fleet once moored. And the masts of sailboats at the marina looked like a battalion of lancers awaiting a call to charge. What was once a working fishing village was now, again, in the waning days of the pandemic, a pretty and thriving tourist trap.

Norm heartily approved of it all and was not surprised to find beyond the top of the hill that the village had spawned a considerable suburb stretching into what were once grassy windswept fields.

Doubling back through town he checked to see if the old Legion Hall was still in the same place, found the local cannabis store, checked into his motel, and immediately collapsed on top of the bedspread.

******

Norm was late arriving. When he finally got to the hall he'd had to circle the car park twice until settling for a spot at its outermost reaches. Though he was anxious to get inside and find Emmy, the fear nagged at him that once he walked into the Legion Hall all of his hard-won adult self-assurance might just drop away like an off-the-rack suit and leave him, in the face of a room full of vaguely familiar strangers, exposed in his old role as his old meek ineffectual self.

So he took his time and sat in the car and rolled a fatty and tried to distract himself from the delirious dread that attended thoughts of seeing Emmy once again after a lifetime apart.

The buds were quite fresh for government-issued weed. Agreeably moist and sticky, if a little pungent for his tastes. He wondered why it was necessary for weed these days to smell more than just mildly skunky. When did it become de rigueur for quality grass to announce itself not by emitting an olfactory hint of Pepe Le Pew, but by reeking of a whole pack of skunks? Wouldn't it be good business to offer varieties selected for having less odour? Or perhaps for coming equipped with pleasant scents like roses, lavender, or new car? He made a mental note to remember this capital idea and to look into whether or not it had already been done.

Reaching for the glove box to see if there was some sort of writing implement inside and perhaps some paper or similar material suitable for writing on - because let's face it, he was never going to remember this idea - he was overtaken by a throat-tearing coughing spell.

Simultaneous to that event was the realization that he was probably going to get dinged when he returned the rental car smelling like a ... what is the word for a pack of skunks? he wondered, lowering the window. A stink of skunks? No, that can't be. It was something else, something that started with an 's' though. It would come to him. He made a mental note to remember to let it come to him.

From inside the hall he could hear the faint yet unmistakable strains of the Chambers Brothers, 'Time has come today, hey!'

The Chambers Brothers? Great song, but not really apropos for their generation surely. He thought the DJ may have confused the Class of '81 for the Class of '68. Still, great song though.

He took a pull and began to sing along, 'Now the time has come, hey/ There's no place to run, hey/ I might get burned up by the sun, hey/ But I had my fun, hey.'

Fuckin' eh.

By the time the song was over he'd decided the time had come to make an entrance.

A table was set up at the door to check in attendees. He took his place in line waiting behind two small round women wearing the kind of flowery print dresses his grandmother once wore. He believed they were called Agnes and Deborah. But he couldn't be sure and didn't want to insult them by asking, so he said nothing. To his relief they chatted together quietly as though he wasn't there. Chatted together quietly while emitting a faint, and frankly odd, aroma of burnt toast.

From within he heard an old Alan Parsons tune. 'Some Other Time' from 'I Robot.' The DJ was obviously working a theme. Far out.

'Could it be that somebody else is/ looking into my mind/ some other place/ somewhere/ some other time ...'

In front of the two frumpy ladies was a tall skeletally thin balding man who he thought might be Brian something-or-other. His last name might've started with a C. His wife was a bronzed, healthy, athletic type with a prominent toothy smile and the endearing habit of repeatedly resting her head on his shoulder to punctuate their conversation. Norm liked her immediately but couldn't recall Brian's surname, if Brian was his name, so again he merely waited and said nothing.

Presently the first couple took their name tags and goody bags and headed through the double doors into the great hall beyond. Norm eyed the goody bags and hoped they might contain some smoked salmon or some good chocolate or … well, even bad chocolate would suffice.

Hungry. He took out a stick of gum and chewed it greedily. Minty. Viscous. Was that the right word? Viscous? Chewy. Sweet. That was the right word. Sweet. Surfeit. Surfeit? Where did that come from? Things seemed to be misfiring in the ol' neocortex. Or is it the other thing? The hippocampus?

He remembered a documentary he'd seen about this railroad worker who had a five or six foot iron bar blasted clean through his skull. Right through his jaw and out the top of his head. Left a hole you could putt a ball into. And he survived too. Amazing. Affected his memory though. Short term, Norm thought. Or was it longterm? He couldn't remember.

Parson's take on time (actually Eric Woolfson's take on time, he reminded himself pedantically, it was he who wrote the lyrics) was followed naturally enough by Pink Floyd's take on time.

Here we go.

Over the song's low intro, the sound of voices, laughter, and chairs legs screeching across the hardwood floor escaped into the foyer, waiting room, vestibule, antechamber, porch, outer world …

When he was a kid this had always seemed a really spooky building, Norm reflected. An old converted Anglican church from the early 1800s, complete with a graveyard of listing, weathered tombstones which always seemed unappetizingly close to a public picnic area. He'd always been terrified of the place. Fearful as a child that if he strayed into the hall in search of his parents during their Saturday afternoon happy hour, that he might somehow find himself condemned to premature burial in the adjoining, proverbial, God's Acre.

What a strange thing to believe, he thought. Wherever did he get that idea? He couldn't recall.

Ah, Agnes and Deborah split off to sign in with Gwen and Kammi, he definitely recognized them, and Norm stepped forward and stood grinning before Laura Dalglish.

She smiled politely back at him for a moment while he waited for her to recognize him.

The moment stretched uncomfortably long.

While it did the idea flashed through his mind that as teenagers we're like a finished work of sculpture, like Greek or Roman gods, as close to masterpieces as our makers are going to physically shape us. And then as we age it's like the block of marble slowly re-engulfs us. Kind of like that statue of Daphne turning into a tree, swallowing up our sharp youthful lines, thickening over our limbs and torsos, until in the end we're entombed, our youth and our beauty as lost as our lives.

But, you know, not so much turned into branches and leaves as such. More like spare tires, saddle bags, and bicep wattles.

Well, maybe the Daphne analogy didn't work so well.

Surfeit. Surfeit of pigs! That was it. A multitude of pigs is a surfeit.

'Ticking away the moments that make up a dull day … '

It occurred to Norm finally, to wonder how long he'd been standing there. And why. Was it his turn to speak? Did Laura say something that he somehow missed? Was she waiting on his reply? He didn't think so.

At last, reasonably sure that he hadn't blanked, he gambled that an attitude of mock chagrin at her inability to recognize him adequately followed the general drift of their conversation up to that point.

"Laura! It's Norm. Norman. Norman Wolfe."

She blinked at him, maintaining her smile. He waited, grinning uncertainly, waiting for the shoe to drop, not yet wondering if it ever would. A spasm of confusion registered on her face. She glanced at the list of names in front of her frantically trying to recall if she'd ever known someone named Wolfe, and oh my god, if she had, is this early onset Alzheimers?

She ran her index finger up and down the list twice. There was no Wolfe. Without looking up she cast a side eye at Gwen.

At last the two frumpy ladies collected their handouts with exaggerated laughter and lumbered through the doors. Gwen and Kammi, finding no one left in line to check in, looked quizzically at Norm, then at Laura.

"This is Norman Wolfe," said Laura, widening her eyes at them theatrically.

They looked at him, none the wiser. Gwen ventured an, "Hm hmm?"

Kammi waited a beat in the ensuing silence and then suggested, "Oh, if you're a spouse you don't have to check in. If your wife has already, that is."

Now Norm was confused. "No, my wife's from away. My ex-wife I mean. I'm from here. I'm Norm Wolfe, Class of '81."

"From Stanfield High?" asked Laura.

"Of course Stanfield High." He was getting exasperated now. "You can't have forgotten me. I don't look that much different."

Gwen uttered an "I ..." then gave up and blew audibly through her lips as though she were exhaling a large toke.

Again they regarded each other in turn, sharing their confusion and growing discomfort.

"Listen," Norm said, "Is Marion here? She'll remember me."

"Marion Douglas?" said Gwen.

"Edwards," corrected Kammi.

"Right. Sorry. Marion Edwards?"

"Yeah. Emmy. She'll remember me. She has to."

They looked at him dubiously while Laura got up to go inside and find her.

'You are young and life is long and there is time to kill today/ And then one day you find ten years have got behind you ...'

"You really don't remember me at all?" he asked. "I mean, I know it's been a long time and I was pretty forgettable, but Jesus ..."

"Well your name's not on the list either, so."

"Who did you hang out with? Who were your friends, do you remember?" suggested Kammi.

"Well, mostly Marion. But I knew all of you. You're Gwen. You're Kammi. That was Laura. I know you all. I mean, we were all friends. I thought."

'So you run and you run to catch up with the sun but it's sinking/ Racing around to come up behind you again/ The sun is the same in a relative way but you're older/ Shorter of breath and one step closer to death ...'

Laura returned followed by Peter McAllister who had to duck slightly to get through the door. He was called High Pockets due to the fact that he'd been six foot six by grade nine and about five and a half feet of that had seemed to be legs. But he'd also been known as Saint Peter because, naturally, in high school he'd been the basketball star, and the local sportswriter thought his remarkable shot-stuffing was like a bad tempered Saint Peter denying access to heaven - qua: the basket. Pretty corny, but what can you say? It was small town journalism.

Also with them was Norm's old hockey teammate Jeff MacKlintock, Wayne Potts (Putz), and lastly, Emmy, looking guarded and a little stern.

Nevertheless, his heart leapt when he saw her.

"Oh thank god, Emmy. Thank god you're here."

"Emmy? My name's Marion."

"Yeah, I know, but I always called you Emmy," he insisted. "Marion Edwards - M. E."

"Nobody's ever called me Emmy in my life and I've never seen you before."

He was stunned, shell-shocked. He looked round at them standing in a line behind the table as though guarding the entrance to the great beyond.

'Plans that either come to naught or half a page of scribbled lines/ Hanging on in quiet desperation is the English way/ The time is gone/ The song is over …'

He searched their faces for signs of a crack in their forbidding miens, some small hint of a smile that would give away the practical joke. For this was a joke. It had to be. Although it was hard to imagine how they ever could have thought it would be funny.

He knew them. He'd known them all for years, even if he hadn't known them all now for years. This was as true as the sun rising in the east and setting in the west. It just was. There was no room for doubting it. This was not fake news. Some things are just objective facts.

His mind reeled. Fuck, he thought, I shouldn't have smoked the whole thing. This is really good weed.

He decided that if he began reciting events from their shared pasts it would surely jog their memories. It wasn't possible that they could all have forgotten him. He'd be the first to admit he hadn't been a central character in their drama. But he had played at the very least a prominent supporting role. He was certainly no extra.

94

Was he?

"What do you mean you don't know me? I know all of you. Or I did once anyway. I knew you all through school. Right from elementary playing Red Rover and Tag and shooting marbles and tossing hockey cards at the wall. I was there with you smoking down at the Trail in high school. Playing Foosball and Space Invaders at the pool hall. Parties at Welker's Hook and Rocky Point. Pizza subs at Luigi's. Movie night at the old community hall. Lobster suppers at the Anglican Church. Mrs. Davis's homeroom in grade six. Mr. Dudley's Greek History class in grade seven. Volleyball with what's his name that Welsh prick who used to diddle little girls. That time on Halloween we emptied a whole fire extinguisher in the cab of Mr. Archer's truck …"

It was no use. He could see that. His remembrances of things past seemed not to register with any of them. He'd thought his recollections would act as Proustian madeleines and spark their own memories of him. And yet the more he talked the more disbelieving they appeared. These anecdotes called to mind for him halcyon days of shared youthful bliss and high spirits.

These same stories seemed to evoke in them only incomprehension, confusion, and perturbation.

And their performances never wavered. That's what really shoved the knife in. They were as one, deep in character. Not a hint of a giveaway, a bit lip to suppress a smile, a twinkle in the corner of an eye, some visible flicker of conscience at extending a joke too far. They merely stared at him with an evident combination of hostility and pity. If this was some kind of put-on he thought they must have all joined some kind of advanced community theatre and become amazingly accomplished amateur players.

That, or they must all really, really loathe him for some reason.

"How'd you know all that stuff about us?" asked Putz. "The Trail, and Luigi's, and Welker's Point?"

"Archer's truck," said Pockets.

"Yeah," agreed Putz. "What the fuck? How'd you know that? Who told you about that?"

"How do I know this? I'm just remembering stuff we did, 'cause I was there. I remember it like I remember your name is Putz and he's

Pockets. Jeff, I remember the time you and Donny stole Donny's mom's Mazda and wrapped it around that telephone pole. And Pockets I remember when you were playing trombone in the band and you unplugged Deirdre's mic right in the middle of her singing 'Feelings.' I remember the first day Marion walked into Miss Ruffalo's French class in grade eight. I remember hating myself because Jeremy had the guts to go talk to her and I didn't. I …"

Suddenly Emmy stepped forward from between Pockets and Putz and said with such pointed venom that everyone turned to look at her in surprise, "You knew Jeremy?"

"Sure. Of course."

"Jeremy Callas?" said Pockets.

"What about Jeremy?" Gwen asked.

"When was the last time you saw him?" Emmy said.

"Last day of grade eight I guess. Why?"

"I want to know how you know him, that's all. I want to know what you know about him."

"I know as much as you know. He was my best friend in elementary school. Then you moved here and we sorta grew apart. I remember he was sick for a while and by the time he came back you and I had become friends. And that was that. We never really talked again.

The only other thing I remember about him was that you said he asked you out and you turned him down. You told him you only wanted to be friends. And I guess he couldn't handle it and freaked out or something. I think that was when he was away from school there for a while. When he came back he'd turned all gloomy and depressed. Then in the summer they moved."

"Who told you about him asking me out?"

"You did. In the library that day. That day when he walked in and saw us together and stormed out."

"I never told anyone about that. Ever. Certainly not you. I don't know you. I've never seen you before. And anyway, that's not what fuckin' happened. Who are you? Why are you doing this to me?"

All at once her eyes were two ponds overflowing their banks. Great rivulets of tears flooded down her face. And with that she pushed through Pockets and Putz and disappeared inside the hall.

They all looked at each other, gobsmacked.

Laura, Kammi, and Gwen bolted after her and Norm made to follow them until an enormous hand stopped him in his tracks and firmly began to edge him backward.

Every community has its proverbial Gentle Giant, and Pockets had served in that role since the fifth grade. He wouldn't hurt the proverbial fly and never needed to. No one was ever stupid enough to take a pop at him.

"I don't know what your game is man," he said now, menacingly. "I don't know how you're doing this or why. But your time is up. You're leaving. Right fucking now."

Norm raised his arms, palms out, in the universal signal of surrender and walked away with what sounded like a piercing dial tone ringing in his ears. His legs were suddenly heavy and rubbery beneath him and he had to concentrate hard to make it to the car. When he reached it he sat inside for a long time trying to make sense of what had just transpired. It was like a movie, just like people interviewed on the news at disasters always say.

None of what had just happened could possibly be real. But if it wasn't reality then what was this? The only other alternative was that he was asleep and dreaming. Or perhaps in a coma hallucinating a parallel existence like Tony Soprano after Junior shot him at the beginning of Season Six.

But that was ridiculous. These were tropes of fiction. That kind of shit didn't happen in real life. What the fuck was going on? He put his head down on the steering wheel and closed his eyes.

Norm had seen a confounding documentary one time about Albert Einstein. Apparently Einstein explained to the widow of a friend that her dead husband still existed on a plain somewhere out in space. Like the events of his life were playing someplace over the distant horizon of the space time continuum, like a television signal from an old sitcom carrying its laugh track and corny jokes into infinity, for ever.

He could just about grasp the concept of a TV signal continuing to exist somewhere in waves radiating away from Earth, moving through infinite space. But a life? The unrecorded, un-broadcast, mundane, multitudinous events of someone's life?

That's just barmy, he decided. And not really germane to the situation at hand anyway.

Norm had never doubted the memories he carried of his time in this place and the people here he once knew. As the years passed and the memories dimmed it came to feel to him that the characters in those memories had ceased to exist in a way. He was not the same person as he had been all those years ago. And doubtless, none of his old friends and acquaintances were either. Each of them, all of them, both existed and ceased to exist synchronously.

Was it possible that these waves or signals or whatever the hell Einstein envisaged actually existed? And they'd been crossed somehow? Or that there are multiple mirror-like universes, and that these whatever-they-ares of their multi-universal doppelgängers have become refracted or deflected or somehow erroneously entwined or merged with …

And then there came a tapping, someone furiously rapping, rapping on his Caddy's door.

Norm shrieked and jolted backward in his seat, fumbling at the key in the ignition, not looking to see who was at the window.

"I'm going, I'm going. It's okay. I'm going."

He started the engine and instantly the car was filled with Paul McCartney's voice singing Golden Slumbers: 'Once there was a way, to get back homeward …'

The start of the medley from Side Two of Abbey Road.

"Hey. What's your name? Norman? It's Marion. I want to talk to you."

Damn. He reluctantly turned the music down. He lowered the window and waited, not looking at her.

"No, get out. I can't talk to you through a door like this. Let's go sit over here."

He shut the car off and got out obediently, wanting only to continue listening to hear 'The End.'

He followed her to a small playground next to the graveyard where his parents and their friends used to leave their kids on those long ago Legion Hall Saturday afternoons of beers and hi-balls and the meat raffle. They sat on opposite sides of a picnic table in the gathering twilight and looked frankly at each other.

"I'm sorry I upset you," he said. "I wouldn't have done that for the world, believe me. I just don't understand what's happening."

"You're Jeremy aren't you?"

"No of course not. I'm Norman Wolfe. I've been Norman Wolfe for fifty-eight years. That much I do know. At least I did. And anyway, you can see for yourself I don't even look like him."

"It's been 45 years. How would I know what he looks like?"

"Well he was blond and good-looking for starters."

"You're blond."

"Yeah, but mine's bleached. It's a work thing. I'm a salesman."

"I thought you might be. You seem kind of Willy Loman-ish. But if you're not Jeremy how did you know all that stuff? How'd you know about what happened between us in grade 8?"

"I told you. But what's the big deal? I mean apart from all this other weirdness. That's what happened right? He asked you out, you turned him down, he went mental. That's what you told me forty-something years ago when you told me never to tell anyone. And I never did, honestly. What's the big deal? Why all the secrecy?"

"But I never told you anything. I've never seen you before."

"Yeah, yeah. I kinda get that I think. But I was right though, wasn't I?"

"Sort of."

"Okay. So I don't know whether this is some kind of Einstein thing where time and individual lives are happening simultaneously across different dimensions or whatever the fuck it was he used to believe. But what happened between you two?"

The light was rapidly fading, but she fixed him with a steady sorrowful gaze and said nothing for a long time. Until he got it.

"Oh. Oh, shit."

A brief unwanted thought immediately crossed Norm's mind. Jeremy was capable of that at thirteen? Part of him wanted to be impressed. He shooed the reflection away.

"Are you seriously not Jeremy?"

"I'm not. I swear."

"Can you prove it? Do you have ID?"

He pulled out his wallet and showed her. She squinted at his driver's license and credit cards and seemed satisfied.

"You're from BC, eh? How long have you lived there?"

"Since after high school."

"How did you know all those things about us? I've been trying to work it out and I can't."

"I'm not sure anymore. I remembered them like I remembered my name. Before. But now I'm not … I don't know. I keep waiting for Rod Serling to appear, doo doo doo doo doo doo doo doo, and announce that we're entering the Twilight Zone."

She laughed.

"I know. It's crazy right? Maybe literally crazy. I don't know how else to explain it. This is all so fucking weird. But I do know one thing. I can't be Jeremy because he moved away after grade eight. How would I have known about all the stuff that happened later? The parties, the pool hall, Archer's truck?"

"That's true, isn't it? Good. I'm glad." She was silent a moment then added, "It's kind of like in The Sopranos when …"

"Tony's in the coma," they said in unison, and laughed.

"Who am I? Where am I going?" he said.

"If you see Steve Buscemi and he tries to talk you into going inside a spooky old house, don't go in. Remember he's Death and the house is the afterlife. Don't go inside, whatever you do. Listen to Meadow's voice in the trees calling you back to life."

"I don't think Meadow's voice would work for me. Do you think you could call me back to life?"

"Yeah. I think I could do that."

He smiled, suddenly contented and at peace.

"You know, all of my happiest memories seem to involve you. All the things I've always thought of as my memories anyway.

I remember once we were driving through town on a busy summer noontime in my old Chevy Nova, really high, and every time I turned the wheel the horn would go off and we couldn't figure out why or what we should do about it. Remember?"

She shook her head.

"And then Louis Cornwall waved us over by the marina where all the boaters were standing around staring at us, totally bemused. And he simply lifted the hood and unplugged the horn. All we could do was sit there, beet-faced, laughing hysterically. And then he closed the hood, rapped on the fender, and told us to be free."

He shook his head and grinned at the memory.

"Oh god, and then we drove out to Welker's Hook thinking we could get away from all human beings there, and we were sitting, mute, slouched in the car, listening to 'Dark Side' I think. Loud. And all at once we both became aware we weren't alone and we raised our heads to look over the door frame and all we could see were the tops of dozens of little kid's heads completely surrounding the car looking up at us like we were a couple of Bonobos in a tree. They were a daycare class on an outing to the beach to peer at sea anemones or something, and seemed to find us infinitely more strange and interesting.

You shrieked and all the kids almost jumped out of their flip-flops with fright while the teachers tried to herd them away to the beach like cats while we fell about the car in hysterics.

Oh, and I remember you laughed so hard you blew smoke out your ears! Oh my god, I laughed so long and hard I actually started to worry I wouldn't be able to stop. Like those people who start hiccuping and go on and on for years and years until they go mad or die.

That might've been the happiest moment of my life you know? I never realized that before. Remember?"

"No. I wish I could."

"Oh right. I forgot. The Sopranos."

They laughed and grinned at each other and it really did feel to Norm less like some bizarre parallel universe and more like shared old times.

He felt a surge of warmth, or adrenaline, or he didn't know what … rapture maybe, flooding through his body. His heart pounded, his lungs felt like they were filled to bursting with helium, like if he let go of the table he'd float away.

"C'mon," she said. "Let's go inside."

AH, PARADISE

Richard Jaeger is having one of those dreams where you're aware of the fact that you're dreaming even as the dream is unfolding.

He knows he is dreaming because he's lying on a sofa in front of a roaring fire, cradling Penny in his arms, and he is telling her that he loves her. She is wearing only a small white towel, secured just above her breasts and reaching down to the top of her thigh. Her olive skin is glowing in the golden light cast by the fire. He slides his hand up to where the two ends of the towel are rolled together, unfurls them, and slides his hand over her breast.

Even asleep as he is, and aware of it, he seems able to feel the velvety warmth of her skin against his palm. He is also aware that his pulse is racing and his breathing is coming quick and deep. In the dream he can feel himself as hard and as smooth as marble pressing against the back of her naked thighs, gently probing for a gap between her legs. She arches her back against him and spreads her legs enough for him to slide through and he feels the tangle of her pubic hair on his shaft and the delirious soft moistness of her ...

"Dick, the fire," she says.

"Oh Pen," he says, slowly, rhythmically thrusting now, "Mmm, yeah the fire, oh yeah, oh yeah, I'm on fire too Pen ..."

"No. Dick the fire," she says insistently.

Something of the urgency in her voice registers with him suddenly and he opens his eyes and looks over her shoulder toward the fireplace but finds that the fire isn't emanating from a fireplace at all, but from their next door neighbour's house. Their next door neighbours from the 1990's, the Ohs. From two former hometowns ago. Their house is fully ablaze, and it's this inferno that is responsible for casting he and Penny in the heat and the radiant glow.

He thinks, shouldn't there be a wall there where the fireplace used to be? And how come the Ohs' place is on the living room side of our house, when it was actually on the other side opposite the dining room?

And then he wakes up. Damn.

He shuts his eyes to the morning's grim reality and rolls over onto his back and coughs. He decides that if he wilfully keeps his eyes closed he may fall right back into the dream where he left off. Well, just before he left off. Back to the good part where he was about to feel himself entering her.

Hell, if he's really lucky, maybe once back in the fantasy he'll be able to just stay there indefinitely.

But it's no use. The morning sun seems to be unusually bright this morning. He can sense it flickering on his closed eyelids. He lies motionless on his back, his head heavy on the pillow, and opens his eyes, rolling them about the room. The white silk sheets seem to have taken on a faintly rosy tint. And the off-white coloured walls of the bedroom too seem bathed in a tawny hue. Strange, he thinks.

He coughs again. A dry, smoker's cough, tasting of a campfire. Blech.

Richard throws off the sheet and rises naked and walks through the open french doors to the patio. To the southeast, beyond the glassy lake and miles of feathery, green-stubbled mountains is the sun, climbing the dawn sky. It is a giant, angry-looking, tangerine-coloured ball of flame.

Also rising in the verdant distance is a long trail of dun-coloured smoke looking like a huge fuse is burning across the horizon. The acrid taste of woodsmoke registers on his tongue again. His throat is sore. He yawns and scratches an itch under his testicles.

"Oh yeah. The fire. That explains the dream," he says aloud, but without much interest.

He yawns again, loudly, like the great roar of an especially bored lion and turns and heads inside for the bathroom and urinates through his still partially tumescent penis.

"How is it," he asks his semi-erect member, "that you can get as hard as a drill casing just dreaming about Penny, and I gotta take god-damn Viagra to get it up for fucking Barbie?"

He washes his hands, chuckling at his reflection in the mirror, gargles the campfire out of his mouth, and then strides out the bedroom

103

door to the landing, nude, and descends the stairs to the main level, his penis slapping against his thigh.

He is alone. His wife is away and the maid won't be in yet. He can walk around naked if he wants to. He can do whatever he likes. He is the King of his castle. The Lord of the manor. The Sultan of the Shuswap.

He reaches the kitchen, turns on the TV and starts the coffee maker. Waiting for it to finish dripping, he stands impatiently, tapping his foot, furrowing his brow, getting increasingly agitated by the absence of the business report on the morning shows now that he's awake and wanting to see it.

Instead all he gets is news. Weather news. Disaster news. Siberia is on fire. Spain and Portugal and Greece are on fire. California is on fire. Oregon and Washington and British Columbia are on fire. Hottest temperatures ever recorded in western Europe. Hundreds, perhaps thousands dead of heat-related ailments. Unprecedented heat waves across the Polar regions. Greenland's ice sheets melting like, well, Antarctica's ice sheets. No change in the weather foreseen. Pakistan is drowning under flood waters stemming from the worst monsoon rains in a hundred years. More Category 5 hurricanes gathering in the Gulf of Mexico … Blah, blah, blah.

"IT'S FUCKING WEATHER!" he shouts at the screen.

He flips through the channels searching for business news, but everywhere there is nothing but environmental hysteria. Even the business channels are on about the bloody weather.

Fucking hell. He takes his coffee and a muffin out to the patio and, after a couple of quick laps in the pool, has his breakfast alfresco. Afterward, lazing in the sun buck naked on a chaise lounge next to the pool he sighs, "Ah, paradise."

Some time later he finds himself waking in some confusion.

Over his shoulder to his left a voice is calling, "Uh, Mister Jaeger? Mister Jaeger?"

He realizes first, that he is not dreaming the voice, and second, that he is starkers. His right hand instinctively covers his genitals as he peers round to see who it is disturbing him.

It's a policeman. He is standing a discreet distance away just inside a gate that leads up to the driveway on the north side of the house.

Richard dimly recalls something about a series of break and enters that have been reported recently around the lake.

"Hello? Is this about the B and E's?"

"No sir. Sorry to disturb you sir, but we're going door to door here, alerting residents that they should be prepared to leave their homes with all possible haste. Just in case worse comes to worse. Basically, everyone should be prepared to leave at a moment's notice if it comes to it."

"What? What are you talking about?"

"People have to be ready to get out sir. Pronto."

"Yeah, I get that," Richard says, genuinely perplexed, "but why are you telling people to leave? Are they armed?"

The officer regards Richard expressionlessly for several beats. He's thinking, this guy is under the influence of something. I don't have friggin' time for this.

"The fire sir," he says at last with pantomime patience.

The fire? Richard points across the lake to the distant fire to the southeast where several water-bombing helicopters are flitting to and fro over the conflagration like immense mosquitoes.

"That fire?" he asks incredulously. "It's fucking miles away."

Even as he says this, it strikes him that the fire seems a lot closer now than it had appeared earlier this morning. He shakes his head, looks across the lake again and tries to focus his gaze, get his bearings, gauge its progress from the brief memory he has of it from several hours ago.

Is he imagining it? Wasn't it way over in the distance before? Far away on the horizon? Or had he just overlooked its nearness somehow? Because all of a sudden it seems unnervingly close.

His head feels light. His mind reels. He blinks and concentrates hard against this sense of confusion. He needs to will himself awake. He must still be groggy from his slumber.

Dimly, he hears the cop answer his question, "No sir, not that fire," and Richard's eyes follow the officer's upraising arm as he points gravely over the roof top to the mountainside toward the north.

"That fire."

Richard twists his torso round and looks up on the hill above the house and sees an enormous mushroom-shaped mass of dark grey smoke billowing up from beyond the ridge top.

Stunned, he jumps to his feet, in spite of himself, and stands gawping at what looks for all the world like the plume from an old A-bomb test.

"Holy shit! What the fuck is that?"

"That's the Hornby Creek fire. It's under ten kilometres from here and moving fast, so …"

The air now begins to shake with the approach of a water bomber. It comes over the ridge slicing through the smoke like a giant silver dagger, or a Sword of Damocles, rumbles deafeningly over their heads down the lake into the next valley where it rises, banks, and heads off further southwest to Deadman Lake to refills its tanks.

When the quiet resumes the policeman, assiduously averting his eyes, continues.

"I'm going to tie this ribbon," he holds up a length of yellow nylon ribbon, "around your door handle. It'll show that you've been warned already so that no one takes the time to, you know. Don't remove it what ever you do, okay?"

"Yeah, yeah, sure," Richard says. "Has anybody started leaving yet?"

"Most have gone. The rest are packing up and getting ready to go. If you have any keepsakes you can't live without you might want to start putting them in your car right now just in case. In fact, if I were you I'd clear out altogether. Immediately."

"So you're saying I don't have to go, just that I probably should go."

"Right. They haven't issued an official evacuation order yet. Right now it's just a warning. You should've got an alert on your cell phone this morning."

"My phone's charging. I just drove in from Calgary last night, so I didn't know about all of this. I mean, I knew about the Bonaparte Lake fire of course," he nodded toward the lit fuse on the southern horizon, "but I hadn't heard about …"

"Hornby Creek."

"Right. Hornby Creek. I've never even heard of Hornby Creek before."

"Well, no one is going to forget it any time soon I'll tell you that for free. Might be an idea to get on back to Calgary while the roads are still open."

"How long til the road is closed you figure?"

"Hard to say. Not long I'd bet. And once you get back to the highway you're probably going to run into the same problems. All the routes heading east and west run through areas in extreme fire danger. Just about the whole damn province is in extreme fire danger right now sir. Or already ablaze. So getting out while the going is relatively good is probably sage advice."

"Okay, but Lakefront Drive? How long you think before it's closed?"

"Hard to say. An hour? Two hours? Depends on the wind. On any more lightning strikes. On the water bombers and what the fire crews can do. Those trees are like kindling standing there. We haven't had any measurable rain for months. And not much snow pack the past few winters either. This could get real bad, real quick. Shit, it's already real bad."

Richard, still cupping his balls in his hand stares up at the ominous cloud and bites his lip. And yet he suspects the policeman is erring on the side of officiousness.

Sure it looks bad. But there are fires every summer. They're a fact of life here. Wildfires happen. A few houses are lost, a few hundred acres of forest go up in smoke. Nobody really gets hurt.

So as the cop hastens away to alarm the residents of the next villa on Lakefront Drive, Richard decides there's probably no reason to panic and therefore no cause to leave just yet. But what he is sure about is that he needs to put some clothes on.

After a long hot shower he dons a pair of shorts and a 'Property of the Calgary Flames' t-shirt and returns to the kitchen. The microwave clocks the time at 11:27. He looks out the window to the driveway. Still no sign of Maria's car.

She should be here by now he thinks. He told her he was coming, or rather his secretary did. She said she did anyway. Where the hell is she? The phone rings.

"Ah. This'll be her now."

He peers at the display.

"Ah shit." He answers it. "Hello Michael."

"Hi Dad. They said you'd be there."

"Who did?"

"Your office."

"Oh, she did, did she? Hmm."

"What are you doing there anyway?"

"Whattaya mean what am I doing here? I'm swimming, I'm sunning, I'm living the perfect life. What are you doing where you are?"

"I'm watching the fires on TV. They look pretty close to your place. Are they?"

"I can see them in the distance, but it's not a big deal."

"Uh huh. And what does Barbie have to say about this?"

"She's not here. And how many times," Richard says, irritated, "do I have to tell you it isn't Barbra it's Barbie?"

Michael laughs. "It's the other way round Dad."

"What?"

"You got it backwards. It's ... never mind. Where is Barbra?"

"Barbra is in Texas," Richard answers curtly, moving to the den and switching on the TV.

"Oh. What's she doing down there?"

"Bagging up clumps of tar. Scrubbing dishwashing liquid onto oily birds. How the hell should I know?"

Michael is stunned.

"Really? She's gone to help the clean-up on the Gulf Coast? I'll be damned. I never thought I'd say this, but good for her."

"Of course she's not you fucking idiot. She's gone to Houston with a gaggle of her friends to spend my money."

"I was going to say, it did sound out of character."

An awkward silence ensues.

"So how's your mother," Richard asks finally, trying not to sound too interested.

"She's good. She says to say 'Hi.'"

"Uh huh. I'll bet she did. Well, since we're talking about Missus Lovelock, when are you going to drop that ridiculous name and take mine again. You're my son. You're a Jaeger not a bloody Lovelock."

"Come on Dad. Not again."

"Yes again. Look who calls me dad. Do you call him Dad?"

"No."

"No. That's right. And what do you call him?"

"Nigel," they say in unison, Richard sneeringly.

"He's Nigel, and I'm Dad, but your kids have his name and not mine. You're my son. I'm supposed to disown you, not the other way round. And I will too, you just wait."

"Dad, come on. He married Mom. He raised me from the time I was ten. He was good to me. He paid for my university."

"I offered to pay for your university."

"You offered me a job in the oil patch with the condition that I go to business school or into chemical engineering. That's not the same thing."

"I offered you the chance to earn it."

"I did earn it Dad. I worked extremely hard and got my degree and now I'm living the life I wanted to live."

"Right. You got a degree in what?"

"Environmental sciences."

"Environmental sciences. Lah di da. What do you do all day? Study newts or some fucking thing?"

"Among other things. It's important work Dad. We're in a global crisis and we're on the front lines working the trenches, trying to assess the damage we're doing and what we can do about it."

"And how much did you make last year?"

"Enough for our needs. More than enough."

"Come on. How much? Less than I make in a month I'll bet."

"Probably about half as much as you make in a month actually. So what?"

"So this is what your petty degree and Nigel Lovelock's influence has done for you. Bought you entrance into the ranks of the middle class. That's some favour he's done you. Well done all round."

"Dad, we're doing very well. The kids are healthy and smart and happy. We have a nice little house with a yard and a garden and a picket fence and a friendly dog. We have everything we need. We're doing great. Really."

"Yeah, you're doing great trying to put me out of business."

"In a matter of speaking I guess, yeah. Over the next few years we've got to phase you out. That's right. It's unavoidable, sorry. All your bull-shit about net-zero by 2050? No one is going to buy it. No one will survive it. Seven and half billion people are about to act in self-defence. Time to retire Dad."

"Uh huh. Do you like a warm house and hot water? Does your wife drive a car? Do you still drive to work in a truck? Do you grow all the food you consume in that garden of yours? Do you take vacations?"

"We're working on it. These are problems, but not insoluble ones. We've got the knowledge and technology and the public support to do what we have to do to survive. All we need is the genuine political commitment to match the gravity of the crisis. But we'll soon have that. If they haven't the guts or the integrity to act on our behalf we'll throw them out and do it ourselves. We have no choice now. Power to the people right on, Dad. Up the revolution."

"Crikey, you had me worried there until you quoted Lennon. The patron saint of hopeless imaginings. I'll give you one of his more rational lyrics: Give me money, that's what I want!"

"I don't think he actually wrote that. But never mind. If humans have exhibited a genius for anything, it's survival. Revolution and radical change is what's needed and it is what we'll achieve. You'll see."

"Spare me your Kumbayas, Junior. You sound delusional. If humans have exhibited a genius for anything it's a genius for predation and exploitation. These are basic truths they obviously neglected to teach you in your fancy liberal environmental studies. But then I guess everyone is entitled to their own truths these days aren't they?"

While they've been arguing, Richard has been clicking through the channels with the sound muted, looking for news of the fires. There is a lot to choose from. All the local channels and the national networks are running live coverage.

When Michael fails to respond to his father's latest provocations there is a long silence, broken finally by, "Dad?"

Richard is reading the chiron at the bottom of the screen on CBC Newsworld. An emergency evacuation order has been issued for the Hornby Creek, Deadman, and Bonaparte Lakes areas. He stands staring at the words, in red alert-red, scrolling across the screen repeatedly, again and again and again. His mind is a blank.

"Dad? Have you got the TV on?"

"Yeah."

"What channel?"

"CBC."

"So you're seeing this then?"

"Yes obviously. This isn't new information. A cop was here a while ago and told me basically the same thing."

"A cop? What'd he say?"

"He said to be ready just in case. It's a precautionary thing, nothing more. Politicians and bureaucrats covering their asses in the event things go sideways. This is just the media setting their hair on fire over the latest 'evidence'," his tone of voice here supplies the air quotes, "for 'global warming.'" Ditto.

"I don't know. That looks pretty cut and dried. That's an evacuation order. That's some serious shit. You better get out of there. Now."

"Don't get hysterical. You sound like your mother. Last I heard the road is still open. As long as that's true it can't be that bad. If it gets serious I can ride it out in the pool. And if worse comes to worse the water is two hundred feet away. I can always watch the show from the boat in the middle of the damn lake."

"Dad, get serious. You gotta get a move on. This isn't something you can put off for some time in the indefinite future. This is no time for delaying. You need to act. Now. I'm asking you. Jump in the truck and get the fuck out of there. Right now. Will you do that for me?"

"Will you have a little faith? Christ. They're throwing all the hi-tech shit they have at this thing. Water bombers, choppers, you name it. Trust me. They will not allow this neighbourhood to be taken out by a forest fire. We've got hockey players living on this street. Stanley Cup winners. Rock stars. Politicians. People who matter. Relax, okay? I'm telling you, it's just typical lamestream media hysterics.

'Oh the sky is falling, the Arctic's melting. Lordy, the polar bears are drowning. What are we to do?'"

"Are you finished?"

"Not even close."

"Mom would want you to get out."

"She did once before that's for sure."

"Will you get out of there if she asks you to? I can get her to call. She would, you know."

Richard isn't listening. The winds have changed and the smoke and ash is suddenly much worse, filling the air and pouring into the house, choking him up. He peers out the window at the hillside above and is horrified to see a huge column of smoke with lightning flashing in it like neon. Flames are charging over the ridge top like troops pouring out of a trench heading directly down the hill across a pine-treed no-man's land toward Lakefront Drive and the vacation homes of athletes, artists, petroleum executives, organized crime honchos, and politicians.

The roar that had sounded to Richard like a freight train and that he'd taken to be the sound of water bombers and chopper rotors is in fact the sound of tree tops exploding in fire, whole acres of standing timber consumed in a fiery gulp of flame, leaping from one parched, sap-filled tree to the next accompanied by a blizzard of ash and globs of molten embers.

Michael, unaware, continues, "I'm going to get Mom to call and talk some sense into you."

"No time for that Mike," Richard shouts, "Love you son. Tell your Mom I love her. Always did. Okay? Gotta run."

He bolts for the front door, throws it open and emerges into a blizzard of falling ash and the smokey gloom of what should be the brilliance of high noon. Instead, it's like dusk or a solar eclipse.

It's immediately clear the road is impassable. The fire is cascading down the hillside toward him like flowing lava. And anyway, his Escalade is on fire where it's parked in the driveway.

Slamming the door he vaults through the house, skidding around corners on the marble floors, and stumbles onto the patio. He looks back at the hillside and sees huge balls of flame somersaulting from tree to tree, leapfrogging down the incline thirty or fifty yards at a jump. Across the lake to the south the same phenomena is taking place as though the Hornby Creek and Bonaparte Lake fires were in competition to see which conflagration can beat the other to the shoreline.

Richard does not even consider the pool as an option. A dim memory comes to his mind of a California couple who snuffed it trying that very same desperate thing.

He knows he has one choice and that is to get down to the dock and escape in the boat to the middle of the lake.

He sprints across the lawn toward the boathouse, but when he reaches it he sees that something is amiss. The door that should be securely locked, and that he'd been steeling himself to having to crash through, is ajar.

He pushes inside and flicks on the lights. He finds the spare key in its stash under the work bench, climbs up into the boat hanging on its lift, and turns the ignition. It coughs and sputters but won't run. He knows without looking that the tank is dry. The thief has siphoned all the gas and made off with the spare gas cans as well.

"FUCK!" he bellows as loud and as long as he can before he is convulsed in coughing.

"I own Jaeger fucking Petroleum," he shrieks hoarsely into the din of the all-consuming flames. "How can I have no fucking gas?"

He'll have to lower the boat and push it out of the boathouse and paddle.

He climbs down to hit the switch to lower the electric lift and open the power doors, when he's instantly plunged into darkness, followed almost immediately by the sound of a nearby transformer exploding.

Great. No power door.

Doubled over by dry, sooty, gagging hacking, he feels his way through the dark and manually opens the door. He can actually hear the sound of large burning embers landing on the metal boat house roof like molten hail.

He turns and stares at his half million dollar boat suspended on its steel harness and realizes with sudden despairing, ironic, horror, that he doesn't even know if it's possible to lower the boat lift manually. And there is no time to figure it out. He is in urgent need of a lifeboat, and yet he will have to abandon his top of the line, high performance, cigarette racing boat to the fire.

In desperation he grabs a life preserver and leaps into the lake and swims madly away from shore, watching over his shoulder as he paddles as the ultimate status symbol for speed-loving, pleasure-crafting thrill seekers is engulfed by flames.

When his arms begin to get too heavy to propel him any longer he stops and turns and treads water watching the carnage behind him.

His mansion is just a flaming pyre. The hills surrounding the lake are fully engulfed. Thousands upon thousands of candling trees, scores of burning holiday villas.

Even hundreds of yards out into the middle of the lake he can feel the heat and glow of the flames burning his face. He looks up to watch the vast columns of charcoal dark smoke wafting thousands of feet into the sky. The inferno is generating its own violent storm front, flashing lightning, whirling maelstrom winds, tossing and churning the surface of the lake.

At the mercy now of the furious forces of nature, he begins to bob in place like a cork, or a buoy in heavy seas. Looking around him Richard is aghast to see the surface of the water is mirroring the flames of the fires encircling the lake. And with the heavy chop it appears these reflected flames are leaping, licking, and boiling all around him.

An unmistakable image comes to his mind of what he is witnessing. One metaphor from the annals of the human imagination that this horror conjures up.

Bobbing there in the middle of a seeming lake of fire, Richard begins to sob uncontrollably as he realizes that he is a helpless captive in a very picture of hell.

THE IDIOT

A summer morning's view from the penthouse suite of a Vancouver hotel. Smog and ground level ozone painting a brown smudge across the sky. The smoke of distant wildfires wafting like fog between the towers.

In the window I catch a reflection of myself staring at the view and am reminded of a dimly remembered TV show I saw as a kid. An episode of Night Gallery maybe? I'm not sure. It was fifty years ago.

A normal person these days would consult their phone for an immediate answer I suppose, but I hate those things and refuse to get one. One day I intend to be the only person on Earth not to posses a cell phone. If I'm not already. So I'll just have to be content in my ignorance, or embrace the mystery or some such thing. In my view, not every question needs an instantaneous answer, or merits technologically tethering oneself to a perpetual electronic tracking device. But that's just my opinion, man.

Anyway, staring out at a rising stop light of a sun puts me in mind of this creepy kid who becomes a huge TV celebrity by making eerily accurate predictions of future events. One day he foretells the world will suddenly metamorphose into an egalitarian utopia of endless peace and brotherhood of men and nations. And there will be an end to poverty and disease too and, I don't know, and end to acne and flatulence and root vegetables maybe. On and on. You get the idea. Paradise attained.

People are amazed and ecstatic. Hallelujah! The kid has never been wrong before! All the Edenic tropes of religion and popular culture will finally, assuredly, play out on Earth as they have in the imagination!

But it turns out the boy is lying, telling a fairy tale to comfort the credulous masses. The show ends with a vision of what the kid has actually glimpsed of the future - a blood red sun about to go super nova.

I haven't thought of that show in decades, but there's no prize for guessing what's triggered the recollection. That's the kind of ominous sunrise I'm looking at. One that seems to portend a future far too few people want to think about, or deal with. Visions of our civilization itself appearing to go super nova as the forests burn and the ice melts and this infernal meteorological phenomenon apparently known as a 'heat dome' sits above the west coast of North America like a lid over a simmering pot.

At some point you know things will boil over. It's basic science. Physics, I think, or is it chemistry? I was never good at science.

I'm here on a pair of personal errands. The first, with my newly acquired wealth advisors. And the second with my equally newly acquired health advisors.

The first set of advisors, who've graciously furnished me with this grotesquely extravagant suite, are keen to instruct me on the need - no, the absolute responsibility I have - to grow my wealth. Because that is what one is supposed to do with wealth isn't it? Once accrued, wealth must be grown, endlessly, like a metastasizing cancer. It's like an immutable law of nature or something. Or so I'm told.

But mulishly, as I'm sure my lawyer sees it, I can't seem to grasp the logical concept of endless growth. I already have more money than I can possibly spend. Why should I want to have more? The answer, as far as I can tell, seems to be, why not? And it comes with the very clear insinuation that to neglect this duty I apparently have as a wealthy person to follow the wise counsel of money managers and invest my capital in the market, is to betray a sure sign of apostasy, or mental incapacity, or sheer perversity.

And so I have been furnished with reading materials to peruse. Financial prospectuses, glossy corporate brochures extolling the virtues of the latest, hottest, surest bet - institutional real estate investors.

There is, it would seem, gobs of money to be made buying up homes virtually indiscriminately, cornering the housing market, creating artificial scarcity, driving up rents, and feeding the ever-expanding housing bubble. It's a no-brainer I'm given to understand.

Everyone needs housing. Employment is high. Historically low interest rates makes money cheap. The more properties the Funds buy up, the more scarcity it creates, which drives further demand of ordinary home buyers and individual investors, which fuels greater buyer mania, more investor frenzy, and ever-increasing housing insecurity. It's a licence to print money. What could go wrong?

I half expect to receive a financial prospectus extolling the virtues of shorting the lives of individual human beings. Surely out there amongst the vast army of nihilists boasting MBE's there's one smart ass who has heard of Jonathan Swift and has crafted an ironical financial scheme based on his Modest Proposal. Never mind selling children to rich people for food, there must be money to be made by rich people betting against the longevity of poor people who can't find gainful work, or afford proper housing, or sufficient food. Such an investment strategy would seem a natural compliment to institutional real estate investment.

But this may be an investment opportunity that will only be offered to me in time. Perhaps they're saving these kinds of ultra-insider tips for when I've signed up for the first part of their one-percenter scheme. They probably have to have proof of my complicity, some morally compromising thing they can hold over me, before allowing me into the most exclusive of Neo-liberal clubs. Like completing a humiliating initiation rite to join a college fraternity, or having to whack someone to join a mafia family.

This morning's itinerary is to begin with a complimentary breakfast in the Michelin-starred hotel restaurant. I believe a Michelin star is the equivalent of a goodly number of positive Yelp reviews. After sampling what a truly fine chef can make of Eggs Benny, I will then be delivered like a valuable, fragile parcel in the hotel's chauffeur-driven Bentley the three blocks to the asset management firm for my consultation.

I've been promised a full day of the most expert financial care and attention by a whole team of the most talented, seasoned, pin-striped, hair-gelled, Ax-Body-Sprayed, market prognosticators. Devotees of Milton Friedman and the Chicago School, and Ayn Rand no doubt. Though they may be unable to explain why exactly.

There are serious matters to be discussed. Wealth funds, and hedge funds, and G-bonds, and T-bills, and debentures, and, I don't know, Krugerrand's and the many benefits of offshore tax havens no doubt. That and the shorting of human lives, I'm betting. I'm sure that's going to prove to be an actual thing.

My lawyer, who is no doubt in line for a substantial finder's fee, is clearly of the opinion that I should be breathless in anticipation. But I'm just pretty much breathless. The haste is all on their side of the equation. The suits are aware that my itinerary for tomorrow involves a bus ride to the rather less grand offices of my cardiologist for a different sort of consultation. The Gucci'd money men will be determined to get agreements signed and fees settled before I meet tomorrow's white-coated brigade.

But I have no intention of making either of these appointments.

I leave fifty dollars for the Guatemalan or Mexican chambermaid to send to her dependent relations back home and head for breakfast. I'd rather make some personal reparations to the deserving inhabitants of poor nations one low paid temporary foreign worker at a time, than invest my money in the fucking scumbags at BlackRock.

In the hall on the way to the elevator I pass two maids and their heavily laden carts. I bestow an effusive, generous smile upon them, and offer a cheery good morning.

I want my bonhomie to convey my understanding of their plight. To acknowledge the awful truths at work in a world where multi-billion dollar international corporations are allowed by unethical governments to get away with paying starvation wages. And that these same morally bankrupt corporations, unwilling to pay living wages to locals to perform these jobs, and ever-eager to combat unions, are then allowed by complicit, ethically challenged governments to raid poor Central American and Asian countries for their young women to provide these services.

Not to emigrate here with their families. No. To grant citizenship is to confer rights and benefits. Health and education benefits. Employment rights. Voting rights. And that would defeat the entire purpose of their malignant scheme.

So they must leave their families and their communities for months at a time to become seasonal refugees, transient serfs, hostages to villainously designed and imposed economic theory. And the vicious circle must be completed by keeping their home nations poor. By employing the International Monetary Fund and the World Bank to produce the kind of overwhelming poverty and desperation required to make possible such a heinously inhumane system.

It's the kind of trafficking in girls and women we see in sex trade workers, and religious child brides, and before that, the slave trade. But now desperate and unlucky human beings of both sexes are transported across international borders to perform work and services rich first world people desire. Massages, blow jobs, hotel cleaning services, nannies, gardeners, farm labourers, donut shop workers, it's all the same indentured servitude.

But now nobody gives a shit. As long as we get what we want for cheap. That's the bottom line. It's their problem if they don't like the deal. Take it or leave it. There are always plenty willing to sell themselves for what the corporations are willing to pay. Just not us.

I want my smile to convey my understanding of the damage this must do to their communities and their families back home. How I acknowledge the impact this must have on their children's emotional development, and how their futures must be impaired. How their friends, families and marriages must suffer their enforced absences. All because of economic realities designed and executed by beings who look like me. Aliens masquerading as humans. But that is a lot to communicate with a cheery expression, and the rictus of my smile seems only to frighten them.

Well, god only knows what abuses they're made to endure doing these jobs. Powerless in a foreign land and probably having had to surrender their passports for "safekeeping." We must all look the same to them. We must all look a threat.

When the elevator finally arrives I practically pry the doors open in my haste to make myself scarce. As the door whooshes shut I guiltily steal a brief last glimpse of them watching to confirm my exit and their safety. I resolve to leave a hundred dollars when checking out tomorrow.

The restaurant is full of tourists and institutional investors. The borders may be closed to car traffic for the pandemic, but the airports are wide open to foreign travellers. There is a trade show going on in the convention centre, and the lobby and restaurant are lousy with real estate speculators studying promotional material supplied by the more exclusive, and ethically and morally flexible, local realtors.

A hostess with a neck tattoo, full sleeves of ink, and multiple nostril rings showing beneath her face mask tells me I may have to wait some minutes for a table. But I haven't really the stomach for breakfast anyway. I've never seen a room so full of dark blue suits and crisp white shirts and expensive looking tans and manicures. I'm out of my usual uniform of jeans and t-shirts and gumboots, but even in my Dockers and Hush Puppies, and with my fingernails cleaned of dirt, I feel profoundly out of my element.

I opt to head for the street instead. I pass right by, unnoticed, my waiting driver, a rather louche-looking chauffeur having a smoke break next to his idling Bentley. He's clearly the man to ask when new in town and in need of primo coke or a couple of girls who will pee on you for a princely fee. But a farmer-tanned rube fresh out of the garden in his store-pressed new duds doesn't even register in his field of vision, and I'm free to join in the stream of humanity flowing down the sidewalk.

At the end of a canyon of towers I can just make out a sliver of blue harbour water. I head for it like a soul lost in the desert hieing for an oasis, starting to reel from the suffocating swelter of the heat radiating off the buildings, along with the incessant deafening noise reverberating off concrete and glass. Oppressive too are the exhaust fumes, and the wildfire smoke, and the skunky scent of cannabis, and perfume, and sickly sweet food aromas.

The harbour promises a good, salty breeze that might provide cool and bring to mind an olfactory memory of home. Not to mention providing the relief of a measure of relative quiet, away from the traffic and the echo and the dense crowds of striving office workers all walking and talking and shouting into their bloody iPhones.

I concentrate on that patch of blue oasis and head determinedly for it, studiously averting my eyes from the scenes no one likes to witness, even bloody bleeding-hearted lefties like me.

Down alleyways and on less fashionable street corners of the city, lurk the stumbling armies of the undead, crazed on fentanyl and crack and heroin, toothless maws raging fierce, wounded grievances. Wretched, spasmodic, despairing witnesses to an alienating world of bewildering luxury and almost inconceivable selfishness and inhumanity. You can almost read in their twisted, jerky, stabbing hand gesticulations a kind of sign language, a j' accuse of contempt for the heartless beings whose murderous neglect and indifference condemns them to living torturous, waking nightmares. The cruelty of it all is mind boggling.

I try not to glance down side streets to catch the crowds of them falling over themselves. I'm careful not to stare at the benighted husks of humans all around me on the sidewalks, comatose in doorways and against light standards inches away from moving traffic on a busy morning's commute.

Despite a cardiovascular system long abused by self-indulgence and an essential ambivalence to long life - or perhaps because of a cardiovascular system long abused by self-indulgence and an essential ambivalence to long life - the sights and sounds and pong of it all leaves me desperate for a smoke.

I want to break free of this Hobbesian nightmare, put it behind me, ignore it behind a cloud of self-destructive cigarette smoke. Blow my worries to the sky as Lennon sang in 'Nobody Told Me There'd Be Days Like These.' Although, actually, I've always suspected there would be days like these. I just never expected to live long enough to witness the actual collapse of civilization. Strange days indeed. Most peculiar Mama, whoa.

I arrive finally at my seaside refuge, out of breath, my feet throbbing, and almost in the throes of a nicotine-deprived anxiety attack. Along the harbour, past a vast marine parking lot of sleek white yachts gleaming in the morning sun, runs a tree-lined promenade.

If I was expecting it to be less congested here, and I was, then I am sadly disappointed. The walkway is teeming with joggers and bikers and roller skaters and amblers and dog-walkers and couples and loners and other assorted health nuts.

Are they mad? I think. There's a heat dome overhanging us like a vast Pillow of Damocles threatening to suffocate us. And dangerous levels of ground level ozone afoot to stifle us too. People are dropping like flies on a paint-sealed window sill. The streets echo to the sound of ambulance sirens. The city has opened up libraries and community halls as cooling centres offering free bottled water and shaded, fanned cots to lie on.

You know it's serious when governments start handing out bottled water and environmentalists don't raise a stink about the ecological consequences of plastic water bottles. And you really know it's serious when conservatives don't get up in arms about taxpayer dollars being wasted trying to preserve the lives and comfort of poor people.

It's a Code Red world, clearly. This is a civilization in extremis.

Go back to your homes you silly sods, I want to yell at them. Don't you know there's a health emergency on? Close up your windows. Crank up your air conditioners. And while you're at it, give me a little peace and room enough to have a smoke in relative comfort without drawing the disapproving stares of sanctimonious nonsmokers.

After all, I'm tired. I don't want a hassle. I don't want to piss anybody off. I don't want anyone to have to suffer my secondhand smoke or the sweet 'n' sour ammonia smell of my cigarette, as strangely alluring as that scent seems to be for we smokers. I don't want to transgress city ordinances against public smoking. I don't want some fussbudget phoning the fire department in anticipation of me possibly not knowing how to discard my butt without setting the city alight. I just want all these people to go away and let me smoke a fucking cigarette in peace. Can I have that much? Is that too selfish of me?

No one reads my thoughts. The crowds do not suddenly scatter. I gaze across the water at Stanley Park. There's acres and acres of room there to smoke without discomfiting anyone. But I'd never manage to walk that far. And with the now yearly spring and summer drought, and the usual extreme wildfire risk, it's not an option any self-respecting human being would choose anyway. Not even one such as myself in a state of acute nicotine withdrawal. So that's out.

Instead, I take up a spot along the railing next to the empty billion dollar convention centre, remove my new Polo Ralph Lauren Microfiber Windbreaker ($168 Canadian, on sale at Hudson's Bay Company), and look round at the view.

There's no doubt about it, it's a beautiful city. Made all the more so by the ostentatious excesses of the mega-rich, I'm sad to admit.

When I was a boy the place had been a pretty dingy little port town set in an incongruously picturesque setting. Damp and provincial and quiet and colonial. And I liked it better that way.

Vancouver was always the sleeper city amongst the garish flash of the more cosmopolitan global burgs. More Mary-Ann than Ginger; Betty rather than Veronica; Bailey Quarters instead of whatever Loni Anderson's character was called.

Now it's got the big tits and the blonde hair and the luxe accoutrements of the global elite cities, and I hate it.

I long for the beautiful but wholesome Vancouver of yesteryear. For a harbour full of working fishing boats instead of yachts festooned with onboard helicopters. For housing that ordinary working people can afford to live in, rather than a safe real estate investment option for plutocrats and embezzlers and drug dealers and oil-soaked climate criminals to park their filthy lucre.

I mean, I'm not a communist, not that there are any of those left these days. I accept that all societies stratify along economic fault lines. Some people will always be wealthier than others just as some lucky few will always be taller or more attractive or thinner or more intelligent, or what-have-you.

But the fact that Vancouver is a city full of half empty condo towers acting as safety deposit boxes in effect, for the world's ultra rich to launder their embezzled loot, or their organized crime profits, or merely to securely stash their money away from the prying eyes of journalists and taxation authorities, well. It fucking enrages me.

We're facing an existential climate crisis, and ever-worsening poverty, and homelessness, and inequality, and civil strife, and division. Democracies the world over are under threat. Environmental and economic refugees are fleeing their homelands in desperation for wealthier, unwelcoming nations. And trillions of dollars that could be put to good use making the climate liveable, making life for billions tolerable, is being systematically amassed and hoarded by an exponentially growing coterie of sociopaths. And for what possible reason? What possible gain? To survive global environmental, political, and economic collapse in order to live out an existence safely orbiting the Earth in a space penis eating shit-potatoes?

I can't be alone in feeling this way can I? I mean, isn't it fucking aggravating that as our civilization hurtles headlong toward extinction so many human beings so gleefully flaunt their blithe indifference to the consequences of their actions? Sometimes I feel like Ratso Rizzo and I want to pound on the hood of the super cars of every unthinking selfish idiot I see, and scream "I'M LIVING HERE!"

Metaphorically speaking of course. What I'd really like to do since I'm indulging in violent fantasy is to fire heatseeking missiles at their private jets, sink their floating party palaces, torch their Bentleys, and bomb their mega mansions.

HEY! WE'RE LIVING HERE YOU SELF-IMPORTANT DOUCHEBAGS!

But back to reality.

Suddenly I'm disturbed in my reverie by the sound of my name being spoken by a vaguely familiar voice.

"Is that George Meeker I'm looking at?"

I turn to look for the source of the voice and focus finally on Bea, apparently looking out at me from inside of what I can only think to call, on the spur of the moment and in my shock and surprise, the body of a woman of a certain age.

I mean, don't get me wrong, she isn't matronly or obese or frumpy, or an old biddy or anything like that. She's just not herself. She's pleasantly attractive I suppose. And stylishly dressed. Even I can recognize that. She looks affluent, certainly. But she's just … how can I put it? More substantial. Ampler. Softer around the edges. Not what I remember. Not what I would've expected to see if I'd ever expected to see her again.

"You look surprised to see me," she says, smiling ironically. "Or are you just surprised to see that I've aged?"

I am a bit yeah, though I manage not to admit it.

There hasn't been a single day in the twenty-five years since she left that I haven't thought of her, or tried to conjure up a vision of her in my imagination. And to be honest, this is not what I pictured. How could it be?

To my mind's eye she's still the dark-chocolate-haired, jade-eyed, olive-skinned beauty of her youth. Of my youth. That's the woman who haunts me. That's the woman who's my equivalent of the Earl of Oxford's Dark Lady of the Sonnets or, I don't know, Don Henley's raven-haired Witchy Woman. That's the woman who turned me inside-out with every emotion it's possible to feel - every extreme of emotion it's possible to feel. That's the woman who managed to make me long both to live forever and to die immediately, often on the same day. Within the same hour.

At this very moment in time, in fact.

So yeah, I think it's fair to say I'm surprised to see her.

I try to look stunned rather than displeased. Which is simple enough, because I am stunned. And I find I'm not really all that displeased.

"Did you think I'd look the same?" she says. "Did you think I hadn't aged because you couldn't see me? Like some sort of object permanence

THE BIG DIOGENES

thing? Or are you just realizing that that old face looking back at you in the mirror every morning is actually you and not your disapproving dad?"

I'm dumbstruck. She is insulting me right? I'm not being over-sensitive here. She's definitely insinuating something derogatory. Now I am displeased to see her.

"I never thought I'd see you again," she says, in a tone that I can't quite gauge. "Especially here. You used to hate Vancouver."

"I do now," I manage to say, in a manner that dares her to reach up and snag my one-liner before it sails over her head and clears the wall in straight-away centre field.

She tilts her head slightly and smiles at me quizzically in something like the way she once used to, and for a moment I think she might just get a glove to it, but no. Quicker than I can flinch she's got her arms wrapped around me and she's sighing into my chest, "I do miss you, you know."

Well now my head is really spinning. One moment she's jabbing me with subtle insults like she's trying to tee me up for a knockout, and the next she's got her arms around me like she's trying to hold me up. What gives?

So I let my arms enfold her and allow her to prop me up.

Before long it strikes me that I may be old and decrepit and hungover and exhausted and desperate for a smoke and misanthropic and well, no need to point out all my best features. But my body still has a mind of its own and it's thinking, this could work for me.

I can feel her breasts crushed against me and she's running her hands up and down my back like she's counting my ribs to see if they're all still there. My hands follow her lead and the silk of her blouse feels smooth and expensive and sexy but in truth I can't discern that many ribs beneath it. I lower my face and nestle it in her hair and my breath in her ear makes her shudder just perceptively and she sighs again and presses herself more firmly against me.

I glance back toward the city and try to recall how many blocks away the hotel is and wonder idly whether it's as hopeless to get a cab in this city as all the Uber zealots claim it is. I'm not confident this growing ardour will survive the trek up however many blocks we would have to walk.

And then suddenly, as though reading my mind, she disengages and takes my hands and holds me at arms length.

125

"You never said what you're doing here."

"Neither did you," I point out reasonably.

"I live here." She nods toward one of the glassy towers further down the promenade. "Right over there in fact."

"That's handy," I say out loud, not meaning to.

"Hmm?"

"For work I mean. You work downtown?"

"Yes, I have a gallery on Robson. Native art. Sculptures, carvings, and paintings. They're very hot culturally. Very de rigueur. No self-respecting collector would be so crass as not to have a collection these days. Don't decorate your home without it, I say."

What is that? An American Express reference? That's kind of culturally inappropriate surely. My body recovers its senses and returns to dormant mode.

"You should come by. You used to collect."

"I was never a collector in that sense. I used to buy it, sure. I like native art."

"You weren't a collector? What are you talking about? The house was full of native paintings and sculptures and carvings. I remember you buying those massive great carved double doors with the ravens on them from Billy when we didn't have the money to fix the tractor. And then having to totally renovate the front entrance of the house to make use of them."

"Well sure. But that's different. He was a friend. We were a community. He bought our produce, we bought his fish and his art. People bought our hay and our meat and our eggs and ate at your restaurant. And we bought their services and supported their businesses. That's what communities do. Mutually support each other. Besides, you have to admit, those doors were beautiful."

"They were beautiful. But we were broke. We didn't need art. We needed a pot to piss in."

"We always need art. It nourishes the soul. It makes life worth living. And we also needed to support our friends and neighbours as they supported us."

"Well, that's what I'm doing. I'm supporting native artists. You should be pleased rather than pissy."

"Who said I'm pissy?"

"You look pissy. You wrinkled your nose at me for having a gallery."

"Did I? I didn't mean to. It's just that what you're talking about isn't really art though, is it? It's more like interior decorating. I bought native art because of the mythology. I bought it because there's an environmental wisdom to native cultures that we could learn a lot from. Collective wisdom that we've done our utmost to suppress, even to literally kill through outright cultural genocide. I just wanted to support that wisdom. I wanted to learn from it. Celebrate it. Improve myself by it."

"What's the difference? When you fill your house with native art it's in the spirit of wisdom and benevolence, and when others do the same it's just interior decorating?"

"No, that's not what I mean. It's just that, when I buy it, *I'm* buying it, because it speaks to me. Because it informs me. Because it makes my life better and more meaningful somehow. It reminds me to conduct myself differently. To live more thoughtfully and wisely. More sustainably.

When some interior decorator buys it for a client it's just because the house is west coast style and the native designs go with post and beams, and cedar, and glass, and ocean and forest views. It's the equivalent of granite counters, marble floors, and gold-plated faucets. All of which are the kind of thoughtless consumerism that directly contradicts everything that native cultures are all about."

"God you are such a snob. I don't hear any of the artists complaining."

"Are they actually natives, or cultural appropriators working in an ersatz native style?"

"Authentic Indians. I make sure. I don't sell anything but the real thing. It's worth more. My clients only want the best. Only the most exclusive."

"Well, as long as they're genuine native artists getting the money, then fair dos I guess. More power to them.

But don't you see how it's just a means of co-opting them? They were our last chance to save ourselves. Our last tie to our former humanity. If we kill them off or buy them off we're finished. Native peoples used to represent something more. They were the last remaining fount of traditional knowledge. Our last connection to an ethos beyond nihilistic acquisitiveness and mindless consumerism.

They want to be able to point to native peoples as just another group who are in on the scam. Don't you see? They're buying them off. One nation at a time. Divide and conquer."

"Who are 'they' George?"

"Capitalists. Fossil fuel companies. Governments. If you've got three-quarters of native nations demanding an end to environmental destruction, an end to pipelines, an end to the Tar Sands, an end to oil and gas drilling, and an end to clear cut logging. If you've got a noisy majority of native peoples demanding economic justice, and reparations for historical injustices, how do you defeat them? Divide and conquer.

You send the cops and riot troops, and vigilante thugs, if you can get away with it, against protesting native bands - uppity Indians as I'm sure they call them in their morning briefing sessions. And you beat them, and threaten them, and intimidate them, and jail them, and sometimes even kill them and get away with it.

And to more malleable native bands, the poorer or more desperate nations, you offer jobs and "economic development" in extractive industries in disputed or native-controlled territories. You offer water treatment facilities to nations that have been poisoned for decades by toxic water and government neglect. Make wealthy celebrities of their artists and cultural leaders, selling them on consumerism as we did selling ourselves on it through our own celebrity culture. Make them complicit in our environmental crimes, our fossil fuels, and our Neo-liberal capitalism. Offer them pipeline jobs. Oil and gas rents and leases on native lands. Give them a small taste of the action like a Tony Soprano or a Don Corleone might. In one hand offer a bribe. In the other offer a truncheon."

"Oh my god. That is so racist. And so selfish. So, what, they should starve to assuage your white guilt and environmental do-good-ism? Everyone has to earn George."

Ah, the racist-old-white-male-privilege ploy, combined with the accusation of harbouring left wing liberal guilt. An unanswerable Socratic argument. Because, let's be honest, there is aways some truth in it. How could there not be? I'm a straight white liberal first world male. Some of the responsibility for past wrongs gets bequeathed to us along with the inherited wealth. Or should do anyway. Whether we like it or not. We benefited by the historical injustices of a rigged system. We may not like to admit it, but it's unarguably true.

"I don't know, maybe you're right," I admit tamely. "It's just that nothing corrupts like affluence. Not even power. Native cultures have a different conception of wealth. They used to anyway. Community, sustainability, living harmoniously with nature. Within nature. As a fellow being of creation, not as a species set down on Earth by an old bearded white guy in the sky to have dominion over lesser creatures. These ideas and ways of living were true riches. I worry we're contaminating them with our own toxic ideas of what constitutes wealth. Handing out cash and consumer culture like we once infected them with diseased blankets."

"Easy for you to say. You're not poor."

"True enough I guess."

There was once a time when I would've been eager for a debate such as this. Roused by the challenge of defending myself against her polemical attack on my liberal bona fides. But all at once what energy I possess seems to drain out of me like water down an open plughole. I find I really haven't the energy for coherent thought at the moment. I'm very tired suddenly. I skipped breakfast. I haven't had a coffee yet. And I'm still desperate for a smoke.

After all, what do I know? Who am I to say what's right? And what difference can it make at this point anyway? We're fucked. We all know it. We're on a runaway train to extinction.

"We're all accomplices now, I suppose."

We pause and glance around at the glinting city and the gleaming yachts and the crowds and I can sense she's searching for suitable words of disentanglement from this dismal brief encounter.

"So once again she asks," Bea says finally, trying gamefully to lighten the mood after several moments of glum silence, "what brings you to the big smoke George? Why am I running into you in Coal Harbour of all places?"

"I was looking for a place to sit down and have a cigarette to be honest. I'm dying for one."

"But you're not living here?"

"God no. Just visiting."

"I thought maybe you'd migrated away from the island at last now that you've sold the farm."

Hello. Excuse me?

"You knew I sold the farm? How?"

"I'm still in touch with a few people back home. Everyone was amazed you sold it. I thought they'd haul you out of there feet first one day."

"That was the plan. Or would've been if I'd had one. It was getting too much for me."

"I heard you made a killing though, so that's alright eh?"

I look at her closely trying to decide if she's taking a shot at me. Is she insinuating something? Accusing me of 'selling out' in the sense of the phrase that used to be interpreted by any person of integrity as an insult. I can't tell. And the confusion only makes me feel suddenly more tired and unsteady.

"Are you okay?" she asks, concerned. "Do you want to sit down?"

"It's the heat dome," I say. "The air is so thick with humidity you could almost touch it like gauze."

She glances quickly around for an unoccupied bench for me to collapse upon. She sees one far off down the walkway and leads me by the hand down a long steep, wide flight of concrete steps through dense crowds of sweat-dripping tourists and unmasked power walkers to a bench in the shade of a small ornamental maple tree. I flop on it gratefully.

"Is that better?"

"Much, thanks."

My breathing is coming pretty shallowly and I concentrate on taking deep breaths. In, one two three four five. Out, one two three. In, one two three four five. Out, one two three.

My heart begins to calm down. I can see in my peripheral vision that she's scrutinizing me as I watch an oil tanker, low in the water, fully loaded with filthy Alberta crude, inching its way through the harbour toward open sea and its long smoke-spewing voyage across the Pacific to China.

Several recently splashed down float planes are noisily motoring toward their docks like murder hornets returning to their nests. Two more taxi away from the pier to prepare for their lift-offs, as another takes off, thunderously gaining in altitude and heading west toward the islands to pick up more far-flung morning commuters.

She's still watching my face. I glance at her, offer a thin weary smile and shrug. Whattaya gonna do? I'm old. We're old.

"Is it alright to smoke here do you think?" I ask, feeling in my wind-breaker pockets for my pack and lighter.

"George! Jesus. Give it a rest for a while," she says teasingly, the way she used to when I was ardently in need of something else entirely.

I get the allusion and we both laugh.

"I can't believe you haven't quit yet," she says. "I quit years ago and I feel so much better. You should try it."

"I did. I quit for ten years or so. And I did feel better. Except for the getting fat part."

"You were fat?" I nod. "I don't believe it. You look like George Orwell. How much did you put on?"

"I'm not sure. More than fifty pounds at least. I stepped on the scale one day, I don't know why, I never paid it any attention usually, and it read 215 pounds. I thought the thing was broken.

I was putting it in the trash when my girlfriend at the time was coming home. She says, 'What are you doing?' I say, 'I'm throwing this thing out. It's broken.' She says, 'No it isn't,' and proceeds to stand on the thing and prove me wrong.

I couldn't believe it. Linebackers are 215 pounds. Hockey goons are 215 pounds. I never stood on the thing again, so I have no idea how much weight I really put on. More than that for sure."

"So that's why you started up again? Because you were too vain to be fat?"

"No. I lost all the weight and then some before I started again."

"Well then for god's sake why did you start again? It's so stupidly self-destructive."

"I don't know. Stress. Debts. Trying to keep the farm afloat. Maybe trying to recapture a little of the glory of glory days, as Springsteen had it. I missed it Bea. It was something lost that I could have back. It was an old pleasure easily regained while all the rest are rapidly falling away.

And anyway, I'm a human. We're all stupidly self-destructive aren't we?"

And then she says to me, "George, you got fourteen million dollars for the farm. You have so much to live for. For Christ's sake you can afford all the pleasures there are. Most of them anyway. And it's smoking you choose?"

ALAN WEBB

Now there are any number of ways she could've known how much I sold the farm for. She may still have friends on the island as she said, though I'm doubtful of that. She may have a real estate porn addiction and saw the listing, or saw that it had sold and, I don't know, rang the agent and asked, or checked the records at some public office that records such things. I don't know. But something about her tone or the fact that I long ago learned the hard way not to trust her made my hair stand on end.

So I ask her, "How did you know how much I got for the farm?"

"My husband bought it," she says.

Honest to god, my heart stops beating for a moment.

"What the fuck do you mean? Your husband is the numbered company who bought my hundred acre waterfront farm and is going to carve it up into a bloody McMansion strata development? Outer Vulgaria with float plane facilities and helicopter landing pads for Vancouver commuters? A deep water marina for resident's yachts? Swimming pools and tennis courts? That's your husband?"

"Well if that's the way you feel, why did you sell it to him? If you cared so much about what happened to it, why didn't you donate it to islanders for use as a park? Or just sell it for less to a local? But you took his money didn't you?"

"I had no choice. I took the only offer I got. And yeah, I walked away with a lot of money. But only after the bank and Revenue Canada helped themselves. I can't believe this. Did you know he was buying my farm?"

"It was my idea."

"Your idea?"

"Hmm hmm."

"Your idea?"

"Quit saying that. Yes, it was my idea. Keep your voice down. People are starting to look.

I thought I was doing you a favour. I knew you probably needed the money. You always did. And when I saw it listed for sale, well. It was such a beautiful property. All that lovely gently rolling, arable land. All that mature timber. All those miles of walk-on beachfront. My god, fourteen million was a bargain. The place was priceless."

132

"It was to me. It was to my family. It was to the community. And you had to go and put a fucking price on it didn't you?"

"I didn't. Your real estate agent did. And Francesco just paid the asking. It had nothing to do with me. I just pointed it out to him."

I am so angry I think a ventricle will explode right then and there.

"And listen to you going on about family," she says. "You have no family. Your grandfather is dead. Your dad is dead. Your son is dead. The father, the son, and the holy ghost have taken the last train for the coast George. There's no one left.

Meeker Orchards are no more. It has ceased to be. It has gone to meet its maker. It has joined the choir invisible. It is a stiff, bereft of life, if you hadn't sold it to my husband it would be growing nothing but daisies. It is an ex-orchard."

"Very funny. That farm was my legacy, as it was my dad's before me. It was my responsibility to keep it going."

"Well, you failed. Nice job."

I glare at her murderously, and she continues in a more conciliatory tone.

"Do you think they're watching you from on high? Do you suppose your old dad and his old dad are aware that you've cashed in the old homestead for a great whack of cash? Do you think they wouldn't have done the same in your shoes? It wasn't worth much in their day. They were just subsistence farmers. They made a few thousand a year on vegetables and fruit and wool and eggs and what? A bit of lamb, and beef, and pork? No one was going to get rich on that. The land was practically worthless. A hundred acre farm that promised nothing but hard toil for little return on a remote island nobody wanted to live on.

But now that land is worth a fortune. It's paradise on Earth. And only very wealthy people can afford to live in paradise George. I'm sorry, but that's the facts. That's reality. That's the way the world works.

So take the money and run. Don't you have a bucket list? Just do it, as the ads say. Hell, buy another place on the island. You can afford to now."

I am absolutely dumbfounded by all of this, though I have to say now I really ought not to have been, given our history. But although I always thought since we split up that I had a pretty good handle on her, could it be that she didn't know me at all? Did she really believe I would be pleased by this, this outrage? Or did she simply not give a rat's ass? Or did she engineer the sale as a way to hurt me for some imagined former transgression? Or merely to be wantonly cruel just for the thrill of it?

I don't know. I'll never know. I've never understood anybody to be honest. Especially her.

"All those years we were together, did you really not know me at all?" I ask lamely.

"Did I know you? Oh my god did I know you. All your so-called 'principles' and your naiveté, and your whole 'beauty will save the world' routine? All your insufferable sanctimonious bullshit?

I practically begged you to give up on farming and subdivide that land. You competed hopelessly with California for the fruit and vegetables market. And you couldn't grow enough produce to supply local chain groceries anyway. Your local market garden was a silly nonstarter on an island where just about everybody had gardens of their own. You wouldn't even grow dope when I suggested it, even though you were good at it and you could've made a mint."

"I grew for friends. Anything more and you risk losing the farm for proceeds of crime. And anyway, I don't like fucking gangsters. You get into large grow-ops you end up dealing with homicidal scum."

"'Gangsters' are just businessmen trying to make a buck like everybody else. They spend a lot of cash in my shop. I know some of them well enough to know how perfectly normal they are. Everyone has to earn a living."

"I know," I say, and assume a Sonny Corleone accent, "I'm taking this very personal and it's only business."

"That's a terrible impression and I'm not sure it's apt in any case. If you want to do a routine you should just stick to your Prince Myshkin schtick. You're good at that."

I don't know what to say to this. I am both offended and puzzled. Offended because I suspect she's calling me an idiot; and puzzled because I never finished the book and could not even know of another explanation other than that she is calling me an idiot.

"Are you trying both to call me an idiot and prove it at the same time?"

"No, I was trying to hurt you cause you hurt me."

"How on earth did I ever hurt you?"

"By treating me like an unethical, greedy bitch. For looking down your nose at all the people who don't measure up to your lofty moral standards. Which basically means everyone you've ever met.

You know, it was Jennifer who first started calling you Myshkin years ago when we were still together. I didn't really get it then, and I didn't like it much. But she had you pinned and labelled. I see that now. You are Myshkin."

"I always knew your family disliked me, but I didn't know they mocked me and called me an idiot behind my back. That would've been useful to know back then."

She sighs.

"You didn't read the book did you?"

"Are you kidding? I hate Russian literature. Who can keep all those bloody endless Russian names straight? Why isn't anyone ever just called Bob or John or Boris? I was lost from page one."

She laughs at this, amused laughter, not derisive.

"Relax. He was only thought to be an idiot. He was an innocent. He was guileless. He believed that beauty could save the world. I mean, I know for a fact you've said those very words, un-ironically. He was also supposed to be Christ-like and non-judgemental, two things that you definitely aren't. But otherwise, if the Valenki fits …"

I'd heard enough by this point. Here I was thinking I was setting an example trying to live and speak and act conscientiously hoping that it might inspire somebody to try and do the same. To, you know, pay it forward in a manner of speaking, or plant a single seed and propagate a whole future garden, or to be the change you want to see. That sort of idea. The kind of notions you see on a spine in the self-help section of a bookstore, or that inform the kind of movie you see on the Oprah channel.

I thought I was acting virtuously. From the best of motives. And maybe I was. It just never occurred to me that I was not only utterly unsuccessful at it, but that I was doubtlessly counterproductive. It seemed to me suddenly that everyone I hoped to influence may have been provoked instead to act in deliberately contrary fashion just to spite me. That instead of making the world a slightly less irrational self-destructive mess, I may have made it inadvertently worse. Not in any meaningful way in the whole scope of things. But just enough to make me feel my life has been an absolute waste of time and energy and good intentions.

"Look George, this naivety of yours, this stubborn obliviousness to the world as it is, as opposed to the world as you think it should be, this was all very of attractive when we were young. I admit it. Your earnestness, your idealism, your anti-establishmentarianism, was all very cute once upon a time. But we're not young anymore. You've got to grow up. The world isn't the way you want it to be. To hear you still raging at society at your age can't be put down to inexperience or immaturity anymore. It's starting to sound like madness."

What is this? Gaslighting? Madness? Excuse me?

"What on earth have I said that equates to madness?"

"George, when you rail for forty-odd years against a basic fact of human nature it starts to sound a little nutty."

"I'm sorry, what? What basic fact of human nature?"

"Capitalism."

I have to laugh out loud.

"Capitalism? A basic fact of human nature?"

"Of course. How else do we survive except by exchanging money or services or labour for goods? That's what humans do. That's what we've always done. You can't argue against it even though you never stop trying."

"That is simply not true. We've probably always exchanged goods for other desired goods, yes. Ever since we climbed down from the trees. We are a trading species. No question. But it's only been the past half century or so that we've been subjugated by the psychopathic doctrines of Neo-liberalism. That isn't human nature. That's a system of economics designed by evil or tragically misguided men. One that is driving us exponentially toward extinction.

To argue against capitalism isn't mad. The Earth is our entire support system. Our survival as a species, the survival of all species, depends upon a healthy biosphere. And capitalism and the so-called logic of the market and endless growth are poisoning it. And not only poisoning it, but preventing us from doing anything to stop them poisoning it.

It is not rational to put the profiteering rights of fossil fuel corporations, and banks, and investment companies and their shareholders, above our inalienable rights as human beings to survival. That is what we have been doing for decades. That is what we absolutely must stop doing now. This instant. Before it's too late. To do otherwise is the real fucking insanity."

"God grant me the serenity to accept the things I cannot change, the courage to change the things I can, and the wisdom to know the difference."

"The Serenity Prayer? You know who was a big fan of that? Ayn fucking Rand. That says it all."

"The world is what it is George. We can't change it. Certainly you can't change it. So take your profits and go enjoy yourself. Move to Maui. Buy season tickets to the Canucks. Grab some happiness before it's too late."

"Bea, for fuck sake, we need to have the courage and the wisdom and the sanity to try to change the things we must change to avert extinction."

I shift myself on the bench to face her, and clasp her wrist in my skinny hand like a grey-bearded loon, and speak to her like I'm some kind of Ancient Mariner.

"Grab some happiness before it's too late? Is that what you said? How? It may be too late already. Look around. Look at us breathing in wildfire smoke, sweltering under a heat dome, in the middle of yet another months-long drought. With a global pandemic raging. The world is on fire. The climate is breaking down. Any year now we'll see crop failures, and seafood harvests collapse, and mass starvation, and masses of climate refugees and armed conflict, and god only knows what else.

At some point all these disasters one after another will surely cause the insurance companies to fail, and that will crash the banks, and the entire financial system. The next disaster may be the straw that breaks the back of capitalism. Or the one after that. We simply don't know when it will happen. But it will. It could happen next month or next year or after the next American election. But it will happen Bea. And when it does, that will bring about the collapse of central governments and nation states, and modern society itself.

And how happy are you going to be then, Bea? You think there'll be a market for your interior decorating doo-dads when our lives look like a Cormac McCarthy novel?

Let me tell you something Bea, capitalism is not a fact of human nature. It is a paper thin economic theory perverted by Neo-liberal sociopaths and fascists into a vast, global pyramid scheme. And it will be blown away by climate change and made extinct long before we are. Climate breakdown is coming for all of us. But it's coming for the fossil fuel companies, and for the billionaires, and for the dictators and the fascists and the strongmen too. Capitalism will be dead before we are, well, before you are at any rate. You'll see."

She takes hold of my hand, removes it from her wrist, and holds it between both her hands, caressing it soothingly, and looks at me fondly. Her eyes are like two small jade stones half submerged in a clear shallow stream.

"You see? You get yourself all wound up and before you can help it you're envisioning doomsday scenarios. You've always been this way George. You forget, I know you. No one has ever known you as well as I did. Things will work out. They always do. You'll see. Go see the world. Travel. Go spend some money. Buy a '57 Chevy. You'll feel better. Trust me."

I can't help but grin at this beautiful silly person.

"You know me? I don't think that can possibly be right, because I have no idea who the hell you are," I say, with more pique than I intend.

"Okay George. Whatever. But I know something else about you," she says pacifyingly. "I know you mean well. I also know that one day you'll see that I did too."

"You said yourself that I'm naive, so the odds are favourable."

I wince. Even to me that sounds pathetic. It's nowhere near the liner I intended would sail over her head. It's more like a grounder, a two-hopper, right back at the mound.

She doesn't offer a riposte, but looks me knowingly in the eye, and smiles sadly.

Her phone rings. Something cloying and familiar. That Celine Dion, Titanic atrocity maybe. Perfect.

"I'm late. I really have to go."

138

She leans in and kisses my cheek.

"Goodbye George."

"Yup."

She walks away.

I light up a smoke. Finally. Nobody cares. Nobody pays me any attention.

After I finish my cigarette I wander down the promenade to The Bayshore Hotel.

When I was a kid I remember Howard Hughes rented an entire floor and lived there for, I forget how long. A couple of months or so I think. It was front page news here of course. But around the world too. Howard Hughes is living where? In Vancouver? In Canada?

At the time, it was a source of enormous pride for me. From then on my city, well, not my city exactly but the one closest to where I lived, bore the imprimatur of the great and famous Howard Hughes. Brilliant inventor. Aviation pioneer. Hollywood mogul. Fucker of starlets. Naked hairy guy pissing in empty milk bottles. The first celebrity billionaire.

It put Vancouver on the map as the saying goes.

Thanks a lot Howard.

I make my way slowly back to the hotel. At an intersection I see an old white guy like me in a cherry red Ferrari waiting for the light. He's listening to the Beatles. The White Album. Very loud, the music echoing off the surrounding towers. Revolution 1. The slow bluesy version.

Just as the light turns green I hear John express his ambivalence toward violence as an agent for profound social change.

'When you talk about destruction/ Don't you know that you can count me out/in …'

I laugh and the old rich guy roars away.

Fucking idiot.

GRAVEYARD SHIFT

I was working the graveyard shift on a really ugly night. The store I worked in was one of a very few in the city staffed by a lone clerk working overnight from 11 to 7. The economics argued against employing a second clerk. The area was rundown, out of the way, not a centre for profitable late night commerce. Patronage at that hour tended to come from brewery workers on break from the neighbouring Labatts plant, and corrections officers picking up grim lunches on their way to their shifts at the nearby penitentiary.

We were also on the switchback route for clubbers returning to the suburbs from the downtown entertainment district. Those trying to avoid high traffic streets and police roadblocks inevitably passed by as they neared the bridge to cross the river. A bracing cup of bad coffee and a stale hoagie were often thought conducive to getting through a road check if need be, while attempting to merge onto the main artery where cops invariably congregated.

The rain had been teeming down for hours, days, and people out and about were scarce.

Directly on the right as you entered the store was a magazine rack and then the till. We weren't supposed to let people loiter there reading. A surprising number of people seemed to want to do that in the middle of the night. I'd usually give them ten or fifteen minutes before gently shooing them away. It ain't a library Bub.

But this night was so awful and the homeless guy hiding from it so pitiful I let him hang out there reading Sports Illustrated and Architecture Digest for an hour or more. I think we talked a little. He seemed a decent enough bloke so I let him be while I listened to the radio, drank coffee, chain-smoked Export A's, and dealt with the occasional drunken customer.

One of the ways the corporation taught its clerks to combat theft is to keep the products squarely stacked at the front of the shelves. When an item is sold the first chance you get you're supposed to go and bring forward the next tin, box, or package to fill the space. That way, if there's a gap, like a missing tooth, and you haven't sold that item, someone has likely pocketed it.

At some point around one or so I was selling Wonderbars and shrivelled, hours-old hot dogs to bar crowd stoners when the homeless guy moved from the magazine rack to one of the aisles stage right, like he meant to buy something. I doubted he had any money.

When the revellers left he came up to pay for some trivial thing like a pack of gum with a handful of coins. But when I glanced at the aisle he'd been browsing in I noticed there was a tooth missing. A can of tuna. A tin of devilled ham. Spam spam spam spam. Whatever.

I don't recall exactly what I said or how I phrased it, but I think I suggested he put it back. Probably with a little too much 'tude, as the kids say.

He immediately lost it. Started yelling that he was going to fucking kill me. He may have taken a swing at me over the counter too, something like that, because by the time he'd gotten all the way to the back of the store to where the clerk's entrance behind the counter was, I was already on the phone to 911 giving the girl what I was sure was a description of a murder suspect (six-two, two hundred pounds, unshaven, crazy eyes, long green army surplus-style trench coat) - he was that mad.

I seem to remember there were still a couple of people in the store too. Maybe a middle-aged Asian guy amongst the magazines screaming "Hey, hey, hey, hey!" Possibly some stoned teenagers enjoying the late night freedom afforded to those kids blessed with benignly neglectful parents, stuffing their pockets with M&Ms while the loser shop clerk is under attack.

Anyway, the 911 operator and the presence of witnesses caused him to stop a few feet short of me, turn and walk out the door just as the cops were pulling up to the curb. Amazing timing. They must have been at Robin's Donuts down the block. They hauled the guy into their cruiser, the witnesses melted away into the rain, and I was left alone in the store on a dark and stormy night, pretty freaked out.

After he'd gone though I realized I was wrong. I don't remember how exactly. Maybe I recalled selling that missing tooth to someone else. Or maybe it occurred to me that I'd been busy smoking and listening to Rock 101 and hadn't bothered filling the gaps since I started my shift. But in any event, I had falsely accused the guy of being a thief. No wonder he'd been so mad.

Between, say, three-thirty and five there were generally few if any customers in the store. Outside would be dead as well. Not many souls trudging past on the sidewalk. None but the occasional car piloted with either suspiciously excessive caution, or tell-tale recklessness moving in the street. So that was the time when it was safe to go into the cooler at the rear of the store and re-stock the milk and pop and frozen foods. If some drunk or insomniac wandered in a buzzer would sound and I'd come out and deal with them.

Around four-thirty or so the buzzer went off and I stepped out of the cooler and walked to the front of the store to find the homeless guy.

He was closer to me than I was to the phone. I had nothing but a pricing gun to serve as a defensive weapon. There wasn't a pair of ears to hear or eyes to witness for blocks. There wasn't anything astir outside but sheets of rain and running streams of dark puddling water.

Shit. I realized at once that I was going to fucking die for naively acting as a rare conscientious graveyard 7-11 employee.

He stood by the till and watched as I took off my coat and made my way around the counter to the cash register. He didn't move or say anything. Just stood there. I lit a smoke, glancing out to the street for signs of life or the cavalry, and tried to look like a kid possessed of well-honed fighting skills who'd long awaited a chance to put them into action.

As it happened, if that had been at all true I would've been disappointed. He apologized for losing his rag earlier and left.

I don't remember if I told him that I realized he'd been innocent. I hope I did.

I don't think I did.

That was the last shift I worked as a convenience store clerk. I quit that morning at the seven o'clock shift change and within days was right back living in the little one silo prairie town I thought I'd escaped from. It felt a bit like if Steve McQueen, having made the great escape, had decided after all that, "Nah, I'm not liking it out here," and tunnelled right back into Stalag Luft 3.

That was a pretty consequential event in my life as it turned out. And oddly one I'd completely forgotten about until today. I was talking to my old school friend Trevor, who did escape into the world, and he casually referenced the homeless guy anecdote I apparently regaled people with afterward. I thought at first he must've been confusing me with someone else.

But no, gradually it came back to me how I ended up here. It almost gives me vertigo to think how one's fate can turn on such a mundane event. Your whole life, the only one you're going to get, hinged on a forgettable incident featuring faceless people whose names you never knew. It makes me feel like a subject in one of those Edward Hopper paintings. No wonder I always liked them. I never fully understood that before either.

I was going to say here, don't you find you spend your life trying to figure out how the world works and how you might fit into it until you suddenly discover you've gotten old and are still none the wiser?

But that's not right at all. The thing is it never occurred to me to try to figure out how the world worked and how I might fit into it until I was old. I just floated along with life like it was a river and I was on an inner tube, kicking back, enjoying the ride. Which is one way to do it I suppose. But it's really not good enough is it? It's kind of irresponsible. If enough people do that pretty soon you get a vast river of devil-may-care idiots fecklessly riding the flood unaware there's a waterfall up ahead.

And by the time you see it coming, it's way too late.

EASTER, 2021

I have met them at dawn of day
Coming with unmasked faces,
From sofa and desk among vulgar
Twenty-first century places.
I have passed a withering look
And a finger to my N-95,
My contempt an open book
A hint that I wish them un-alive.
Though I may alter my path
From this walk to the other side
Tis they who merit my wrath
For their selfishness threatens homicide.
Being certain that they and I
But lived where society is the norm:
All changed, changed utterly:
When the virus was being born.

That woman's days were spent
In ignorant good-will,
Her nights spent on Facebook
An anti-vaxxer to the fill.
How much dumber could be her views
When young and so credulous,
She believed in Q?
This man did well at school
And he believed in science;
This other his helper and friend

Held for letters a bias.
He might have seen sense in the end,
So sensible his nature seemed
So open and rational in his thought.
This other man I had deemed
A drunken vainglorious lout.
He had done most bitter wrong
Covid safety rules he did flout.
Breathing brazenly so near my face
I'd like to kick him in the taint
While I grieve for the human race.
He too has been changed in his turn,
Transformed utterly:
I hope his lungs will burn.

Hearts with one purpose alone
Through summer and winter seem
Bored almost unto stone
To rouse a silent scream.
The noise that comes from the road
The driver, the sirens that wail
Sounds of construction do so goad
Livid sun the high-rises do veil.
Shadow of cloud on an X-ray
Changes minute by minute;
A portent of the end of days
Harbinger of a new variant.
Pubs and restaurants beckon,
House parties and churches too
However does the sane man reckon
The nihilism of the average boob?

Too long a sacrifice
Can make a stone of the heart.
O when may it suffice?
That is science's part, our part

To reason time and time again,
As idiots storm society's walls
Infestation of Christ and pagan
One almost hopes the curtain falls
On humanity such a cursed contagion.
Wither the enlightenment?
Whence our better angels?
Media's a carnival barker's tent
A society so stupid it appalls.
We live techno-separated
Pseudo existences
Eyes down rapt by screens,
Cleaved not by a virus
But by cynicism ignorance and greed.
I write it out in verse -
Cribbed from Yeats what of it?
The most passionate are all the worst
The best are all forlorn
We've changed the biosphere utterly
A terrible extinction is being born.

THE END

thebigdiogenes@gmail.com

Made in the USA
Las Vegas, NV
05 February 2022

43160547R00089